CW00822749

Also by Rohan

The Passion of Bright Young Things

What's the Matter, Veronica Lange?

by
Rohan

For my sister, Kate

A heart is not judged by how much you love; but by how much you are loved by others.

- The Wonderful Wizard of Oz, 1900.

3:30pm

'Oh *there* you are darling,' Veronica said too loudly through the doorway of the tiny dressing room, pausing mid-stride to lean on the frame and glare down into the small space. Kirsten jumped slightly at the combination of the sudden sight of her client and the inappropriate pitch that had accompanied her appearing all at once. Equally as inappropriate was the heavy, brown, woollen coat she saw Veronica had arrived in. It fell almost entirely to the floor with just the top of her stockinged ankles and glossy black heels showing any sign of a body underneath. It was an overly dramatic reaction to the still mild winter that Sydney was currently in the throws of but choosing to swan down a busy street, in a temperate climate, wrapped in an expensive item of clothing made only for the most Northern-European of winters, was a predictable one from her nonetheless.

'Jacquie Swift's dead,' Kirsten said quickly snapping out of her examination of the outfit.

'Jacquie Swift's what?' Veronica spat back quickly.

'She's dead. Jackie Swift. You know, from *Starman*.' Kirsten fumbled nervously as she pulled out a folded newspaper from a crevice in the couch she was sat in. 'She's dead.'

'She's dead?'

'Yes.Page six.'

Veronica leant in from the door way, pulled the paper from her quickly and squinted into the tiny print. For a moment she was silent, her face pressed hard into the thin, coarse pages and her eyes widening as she pushed it out again to focus more. 'God,' she mumbled, blinking a few times quickly before looking up again to hand it back. 'Well, I can't go to the funeral. I'm far too busy with the show,' she said gesturing to the contents of the dressing room. Kirsten squinted at her curiously.

'Well that and you'd need to fly to L.A anyway for it, wouldn't you? Says she still lived in Hollywood.'

'What's your point?'

Kirsten seemed to only manage a shrug in response, with both of them remaining in an awkward silence momentarily after. Veronica pursed her lips down at her, waiting to be challenged again, before sighing heavily. 'Poor Jacquie, gosh that is a loss,' she said eventually. 'Anyway, last night…'

She wafted effortlessly into the room, appearing to tower over everything in the small space as she wove her way through it, pausing at a chair tucked under a large white vanity and wriggling her shoulders gently to let the straps of a black handbag slide down her right arm and collapse onto a cushioned bench beneath her. She tore at the buttons of the long coat, emerging from its heavy fabric like a lanky, terrifying insect out of a cocoon, to reveal a figure hugging black dress with short sleeves and a high neck line, underneath.

The material looked thick and luxurious, and the whole thing was in impeccable condition, but it clearly wasn't new. Its shoulders stuck up and out, not padded but still structured and its neckline was high and modest. It outlined her bony silhouette perfectly, appearing as if she had been sewn directly inside it earlier that day. The waist was corseted in tightly and the length fell just above the crease of the back of her knee, exposing just a passing glance of the bottom of her thigh. She had pinned her mass of thick, dark hair up loosely with a tortoise shell coloured claw, that even when gathered at the top of her head as it did, still had enough length to trail down between her shoulder blades. It was a deep and very dark brown, the colour that antique wooden furniture turned after generations of the stains of lacquer and it gathered in thick clusters of loose ringlets about her sharp shoulders.

She paused briefly before turning to start on the examination of herself in the mirrors clustered around her that had become her ritual most days upon arriving. There were three of them in total; three floor length types in one corner that when pressed together in an incomplete cube, created a sort of infinite vortex of the reflections of the angles of her body as she twisted delicately about, a further two smaller, circular and heavily magnified ones sat on the vanity which Kirsten had spent countless hours already watching Veronica peer into and fussing over the most minute details of her skin and eyes, then finally the ubiquitous dressing room type, a large upright, rectangular piece of glass outlined in bulbs that doused anyone who dared to sit in front of it with a blinding yellow light.

Gazing into one of floor length ones leant against the wall, Veronica straightened her back and placed her hands on her hips, carefully pulling the fabric of her dress tighter around her already heavily cinched torso. It was a pose she clearly had perfected over many years, her long, elegant hands pressed deep into what flesh was left around the top of her pelvis so her tiny waist pulled in even further. The pressure of the whole act pushed her shoulders forward, making her collar bone protrude higher through her pale skin and if she angled the right side of her jaw up slightly, her entire body contorted into the almost impossible stature of some high end, fiberglass mannequin.

She was by no means tall, possibly five foot six in heels, but the whole pantomime of the way she moved, her posture, the shoes and the very specific and deliberate cut of her clothes, all contributed to an impressive illusion of some significant height. Even at seventy five years of age, the whole process made her seem tall. Too tall for the space she now stood in. Like an adult walking through a child's room, ogling at miniature versions of a grown up's things.

'What a night, right?' she said into the mirrors, not making eye contact with Kirsten.

'What?'

'Wasn't it just the most fabulous night?'

'Oh, sorry,' Kirsten laughed awkwardly, before pulling out her phone to fidget with. 'Yes.'

'The show of course, I mean. But afterwards also. That party,' Veronica continued fussing about with her hair. 'I must have lost you at some point. I don't think I even saw you once we got to the bar. Wasn't it just the most perfect venue to go and celebrate? All that gold trimming and red velvet everywhere. And those chandeliers too. So lush. Honestly darling, you missed out.'

'I was there.'

'Really?'

'I was with the stage crew, on the balcony.'

'Oh, well,' Veronica smiled and folded her arms to lean against the door frame. 'That's nice, I guess.'

'But well done again. For an opening night, I think it went really well.'

'Yes we did it darling. It feels good doesn't it? I can tell you now, it feels so good to be back up there, those hot lights just y'know, blasting down on me again darling. All those people out there in their seats in the dark, wide eyed and eager, hanging on to every line, just waiting for the next story to come. And the applause, darling, did you see?'

'See what?' Kirsten asked, her knee bouncing nervously.

'*See what?* See what, she says. The standing ovation, darling. The whole bloody theatre on its feet, clapping like seals. That's what. Did you see that?'

'Well, I was in the wings. I watched the whole thing from the wings.'

'There you go, right? A whole theatre, on its feet, clapping and cheering, for me. After all these years, pulling a crowd like that still. There's steam left in some of us old girls after all,' she beamed.

'Weren't you and Jacquie Swift the same age' Kirsten asked mindlessly.

'What?'

'Yeah, let me check.' She snatched the paper from the couch again and peered into the print. 'Yeah says here. Seventy-five.'

Veronica cleared her throat and folded her arms defensively. 'Well, I'm sure she was sick or something.'

'Nope. Heart attack.' Kirsten flicked the paper to the space beside her and shrugged again. Veronica peered down at it, but didn't move.

'I guess they'll want me to say something too, won't they?' She said eventually, sounding flat.

'Who will?'

'The press. We should prepare some sort of statement maybe for when the press calls. Because we know they will. Something sweet you know?' Kirsten nodded and returned to glaring mindlessly at her phone.

'You were friends?'she asked.

'Yes darling of course.'

'Ok, I'll ah, make a note.'

'They will probably want people to comment about the time and everything else.'

'What time?'

'Our time in Hollywood darling. Mine and Jacquie's.'

'Right.'

'God she was beautiful. This tall, tanned, blonde thing from the middle of nowhere in Western Australia of all places, plucked from the desert and rushed off to Hollywood. This jawline that looked like it was made with a spirit level or something. I mean thank god she was beautiful, because she couldn't act and she had the IQ of a mop. But she was a crowd pleaser. Always managing to get those roles where she spent most of the time in an ill-fitting swimsuit on a beach or standing on some catwalk, or wrapped in the white sheet of a canopy bed. She was netting three to five million a film towards the end and that was in the seventies.'

'Wasn't she gay?' Kirsten asked nonchalantly. Veronica immediately winced, scrunching her nose and shaking her head all at the same time.

'Wasn't she what?'

'Gay. A lesbian.'

'Jacquie?'

'Yes.'

Veronica scoffed and pushed out an awkwardly high pitched cackle. 'No, darling. Of course not. How could she be?'

'I just heard some where that she was a closet lesbian. Doesn't it say it there in the paper, something about having a long term like, live-in *friend* or something?'

Veronica cleared her throat loudly again straightened her back and pushed out her chest, going from languishing casually in front of the mirrors to consuming almost all of the space entirely. 'No, it doesn't,' she said without even motioning to check the paper again to verify.

'OK. Well, was she ever married?' Kirsten asked, sensing but completely ignoring Veronica's discomfort.

'No.'

'Ok.'

'So,' Veronica said inhaling sharply and clapping her hands together loudly, 'that press statement…'

'Yeah, I'll see what I can pull together,' Kirsten said half heartedly. 'Did you two ever do a film together?'

'Jacquie and I? Together in a film?

Veronica spun around to lock eyes with her, before scanning from the top of her hair to the bottom of her shoes, and back and forth once more. Her lips pursed tightly together, curling the sections that had been painted with a bright red gloss, outwards towards her face and exposed the fleshy insides to the world. Her arms, already knotted tightly against her chest, pulled in closer and her chin tilted up higher into the ceiling. 'No darling, Jacquie could never have been in one of *my* films.'

'Ok,' Kirsten mumbled as she dove back into her phone again.

Veronica turned around slowly again to face the mirrors.

'So darling, about last night. What news have you today of the outside world?'

'Well,' Kirsten exhaled heavily and reached for her laptop. 'I think it's still too early for the reviews.'

Veronica stopped fussing with her hair and glared back at her from the reflection in her mirror. 'What, nothing at all?'

'No. Well, nothing official anyway. Some tweets here and there from people in the audience. I am keeping an eye on The Guardian and a few others that I know had people there last night.'

'But it's already after three? How long does it take to write a bloody review?'

Kirsten shrugged and pretended to fuss on something on her computer; typing, scrolling, anything to ignore Veronica's increasingly intense gaze. She saw her wave a long, elegant hand dismissively in the mirror, before nodding towards Kirstens's phone sitting beside her on the couch. 'What about on the thing?'

'What thing?'

'That,' she said stabbing a finger towards her phone again.

'Twitter you mean?'

'Yes. Or the other ones.'

Kirsten lazily picked up her phone and flicked it open, still not making any eye contact. She shrugged after a moment and shook her head, ducking behind her laptop screen once again. She heard Veronica scoff again and peered up carefully to see if she had stopped looking towards her on the couch, watching as her gaze dropped eventually from the reflection and then returned to herself in the mirror.

'How odd,' she said under her breath, before swanning over to the vanity, slinking down into the seat and beginning to drag a large silver brush through the bottom half of her long hair. As she pressed a wide open palm delicately on the very top of her head before her brush strokes started growing higher towards her hairline, it became obvious that she was already in one, or possibly even two, of her elaborate wigs. She took long, measured strokes, starting from just above her ears and appeared to glare directly into her own eyes as she did.

When Kirsten caught sight of her own reflection, positioned in the mirror just to the right of Veronica's frame, she instinctively went to fuss with her own hair but stopped. The tight pony tail of her jet black hair was still perfectly positioned high and neat on her head just as she had done it that morning. The thick dark eyeliner was still clean and crisp around the extremities of her eyes, flicking out in sharp whiskers at the edges and even in the position she was in, still sat casually on the arm of the lounge, her grey trousers and blazer appeared perfectly pressed and un-wrinkled. She pulled her shoulders back slightly, tilted her chin up and squinted her eyes deep into the reflection. For a brief moment, she appeared like some younger looking spirit, lurking ominously behind Veronica, past and present all together in one composition, nearly fifty years of life laying between them and an ocean of contrasting circumstances.

Veronica eventually stopped the slow brushing of her wigs and let both her hands drop gently to land face down on the table. She paused to silently examine the composition of the mundane but still ornate objects before her; a full set of pewter, monogrammed brushes and combs complete with a hand held mirror, embossed with ornate floral patterns and Rococo swirls, a row of red lipsticks lined up in a gradient beginning with a heavy, dark Shiraz to the left and ending with something resembling a highly polished Ferrari on the right, several bottles of the same perfume and a box roughly the size of stick of butter that had the same patterns and was of the same metal as the combs and brushes. 'Check that paper darling would you?' she said breathlessly, repositioning one of the heavy brushes and staring satisfyingly down at the bench. 'There must be at least a passing mention of the show in there. Christ knows there wasn't anything else going on this bloody city last night.'

Kirsten reached over again and held the paper beneath her face. She peeled back the pages so they returned to their monstrous broadsheet size and scanned up and down the columns, folding it back down once and then once again and before bringing it into her face. 'Ok yes, there's something here.'

'Great. There's some civility left in the world still then it seems. Read it for me daring, would you?' Veronica asked, as she started to finger the objects on the desk beneath her delicately again. Kirsten fell into the back of couch, crossing her legs, raising the paper up high and cleared her throat.

'Seventies screen siren, Veronica Lange's one woman show *My Life in Pictures* opened last night at the East Sydney Palladium. As the title suggests, the production is a romp through her glittering career in a Hollywood golden age of cinema covering all her greatest hits such as...' Kirsten paused for a moment scanning, waving her hand. 'Etc, etc. Lange talks us through the journey using a selection of ten iconic images of her life *in pictures* showing her on set, at various parties, awards ceremonies, with other celebrities, traveling and at home. It's a tantalizing peek behind the curtain into a world most of us could only dream of. *My Life in Pictures* has a limited run of three weeks from October...' Kirsten trailed off letting the newspaper drop to rest on her lap. She looked up to see Veronica staring back at her eagerly.

'Well,' she said sharply. 'Better than nothing I guess.'

'The actual reviews will come soon. I've got alerts set on my phone.'

'Right,' Veronica sighed, letting a brief, exhausted silence fall between them. She pulled a single ringlet of hair back with her middle finger and pursed her lips into the mirror, before leaning forward and placing her hands into a prayer. 'But,' she said loudly. 'We sold out, didn't we? Tell me we sold out in the end?'

'We sold out.'

Veronica squealed and raised both her hands to her face before turning them into fists and slamming them onto the table excitedly. The little city of bottles and canisters on the bench beneath her shook, sending a gentle symphony of tinkling glass echoing about the room. 'I knew it! I tried to look but I couldn't see anything under those damn lights. But I could sense it. I could hear it when they were clapping. I knew it.'

Kirsten watched her glaring around the room, beaming like a child on their birthday watching a table stacked with gifts. Her smile was wide, pushing the balls of her cheeks up, almost completely obscuring the bright green of her huge eyes.

'Now we just gotta keep it up for the next three weeks, right?' Kirsten said mindlessly. But just as she went to bury herself in her phone again, she realised instantly a tense silence had again descended upon the small room and nervously she looked up.

'And why couldn't we to do that?' Veronica asked, her wide smile now collapsed into an unimpressed, horizontal line and the full breadth of her eyes now dilated and focused.

'No reason,' Kirsten shot back. She heard Veronica exhale deeply and realised she had been holding her breath for the brief moment before she spoke. They locked eyes quickly and Kirsten steadied herself, but when she saw Veronica turn to face the mirror again, she relaxed again.

'Y'know I got given so much material when I decided I was going on stage again darling,' Veronica said.

'I remember.'

'All that Tennessee Williams, Noel Coward stuff with those self indulgent stories about those awful, tragic, fallen female characters that only women my age get lumped with. Sunset Boulevard and Sweet Bird of Youth, Blanche Dubois and Margot Channing. All of them and all of that. And then the nerve of people to raise their eyebrows, men mostly of course, when I questioned why that's all there was? And the eyebrows again when I finally said no. And then when I said, I'll write something myself. *My* story. *My* way. Don't do it Von, they said. Don't sell yourself for cheap thrills, they said. Stick to acting. Don't pull back the curtain or ruin the facade. Bask in your legacy. Fade away with dignity, is what they really meant. Sit in my house and glare out the window at the world as it goes on without me, is what they really meant. But no darling, all those seats filled last night. It's all worth it now. It's what they all wanted in the end wasn't? The people. All they wanted was Veronica Lange,' she said swiping her hands across the air in front of her. 'On stage. One night only.'

'For three weeks,' Kirsten said.

'One night only, for three weeks. One night to catch her back in all her glory, before she disappears again like…' Veronica paused with her hand outstretched glaring into nothing. She turned to Kirsten who was watching curiously.

'Like, what?' she asked eventually.

'What are those flowers that only blossom at midnight every twenty years or something?'

Kirsten shrugged. 'Anyway, them. Catch her before she retreats back into the darkness again.'

'But it's still not a *comeback*, though right?' Kirsten said, using air quotations.

'No. Of course not.'

'Got it.'

'Comeback from where darling? Where did I go? Tell me. What am I coming back from?'

'I don't know, you said retreat into the darkness *again*, just then I thought you-'

'It was figurative.'

'Ok.'

Kirsten glared at Veronica for a moment, appearing briefly hesitant to speak again. She dove into her phone, letting her finger flick softly against the glass, before glancing up again. 'So what did you think about the crowd last night?'

Veronica turned around slowly and squinted at her. 'You mean besides it being totally sold out?'

'Besides that.'

'Well shit darling, I don't know what else then?' Veronica said sharply, spinning around to look at herself in the mirror again. 'They were wonderful. Responsive. Adoring. What more could you want?' She paused briefly, raising a finger up to tap on the edge of her chin gently as she thought deeper. 'Oh, there was that enormous drag queen though in the front row, blocking everyones view. Did you see?'

'Yes, but anything else maybe you noticed also?'

'Besides a ten-foot tall man in three wigs? No darling, nothing else.'

'Right, well, something I noticed was that the audience last night was actually mostly men.'

Veronica reached over and plucked a lipstick from the row of canisters against the mirror and puckered her lips into the glass. Before she touched it to her face, she leant in and winked at Kirsten. 'Well, y'know, nothing wrong with that is there?' Kirsten smiled again, this time failing entirely to hide the strain behind it. 'But who cares,' she shrugged. 'As long as it's full, right? What does it matter who is sat out there in the dark?'

'Well it's always good to know who your audience is.'

'I've always known who my audience is.'

'Do you know who they are now though?'

'Darling what are you on about?' Veronica sighed, finishing the lipstick job off with the tip of her finger. Kirsten sighed and rubbed her face aggressively with her both her hands. 'It's men,' Veronica said. 'It's always been men. Women have never taken to me. Producers have always said that. Men come to watch. Women come to observe. Assess. Examine. Critique.'

'Yes but I think it might be a certain kind of man, now.'

'What do you mean *now*?'

Hesitating, Kirsten placed her phone down on the couch and held her hands together tightly, breathing in slowly. 'Well, it seems to be gay men. The audience last night was mostly, gay men. If not all of it.'

She watched as Veronica immediately stopped fussing with the items on her bench then turned her head to glare intensely into an empty space on the floor beneath her. Kirsten opened her mouth to speak again, but when she saw Veronica turn around to face her, she held her jaw tightly shut. She saw the look that had descended across her face was a mixture of disbelief and repulsion. A look that made her chin snap quickly back towards her neck and her eyes squint like she was shielding herself from some vicious smell. 'Don't be so ridiculous,' Veronica said, wincing. 'How could you even tell something like that?'

'Well, because I was out in the foyer at intermission while they were all sipping their overpriced chardonnay. I saw it. And I heard it.'

Veronica shook her head manically, still appearing to try and clear the non-existent smell from her nose before turning to face the mirror once again. She plucked a stick of mascara from the bench and leant forward, widening her eyes and pushing her eyebrows to the top of her forehead. Kirsten watched and was momentarily impressed with how much movement she still had left in that part of her face. 'Well I think that's very presumptuous of you. I thought your generation was supposed to be past all that? Labels and whatnot.'

'It's not really what I was getting at.'

'Honey, like I said, it's *always* been men.'

Veronica wasn't looking at Kirsten anymore through the glass of the mirror. She was totally consumed in the remainder of the routine of topping up the already heavy amount of makeup she had seemingly put on earlier that day. Slowly and meticulously she combed the tiny bristles of the stick coated in black ink through her own oversized, synthetic lashes, curling them up towards the ceiling, forming them into dark inverted waves about to crash into her eyelids.

'Anyone call before I got in?' she asked, flicking her wrist one last time and sighing loudly as some indicator she was done with the topic. Kirsten sunk back into the couch and returned to glaring into the screen of her laptop once again.

'Your daughter apparently tried to reach you. And your ex-husband also. Reception left your messages.'

Veronica scoffed, sitting back from the mirror, managing to blink and roll her eyes at the same time. 'See this is why I don't walk around with that phone.'

'It would be a lot better for me if you did.'

'That would have completely ruined my morning.'

'A phone call from your daughter?'

'Yes. Did she say what she wanted?'

'No, only that she would try you again soon.'

Veronica flipped open the small silver box on the vanity and produced a cigarette and a heavy looking, metal lighter with more intricate floral patterns engraved on its case. She tapped it on the table gently and fondled it for a moment, staring blankly into the other side of the room. 'Funny how they both managed to call within a few hours of each other. And on today, of all days. It must be at least a month, two maybe even, since I heard anything from either of them.'

'Maybe just to wish you well?'

'No, if that were all it was, then it would have been last night, wouldn't it? Opening night.'

'I guess so,' Kirsten mumbled. 'Were you expecting them to come?'

'I would have fallen off the stage if they had. Danny maybe, only because he would go to the opening of a toilet seat these days. But if they are going to go through the pain of picking up the phone to call me, why not last night?' Kirsten smiled sympathetically and shrugged. 'I'll tell you why,' Veronica said, pointing at Kirsten in the mirror. 'Because they saw it was a success. They saw it was sold out. They couldn't have seen the reviews obviously, you said they weren't out yet. But they would have heard. Danny, I know still sees people we were friends with when we were married. They would have told him. Called him and asked how it was. Asked him how he could have missed it? How if, like he seems to enjoy telling people, we are still *so* close?'

She placed the cigarette in her mouth and let it dangle precariously from her lips while she straightened things once again on the bench beneath her. 'I wouldn't call them mutual,' she continued, speaking now from the side of her mouth. 'Because they were *my* friends. People *I* worked with. Directors, actors, writers. He became friends with *my* friends and then stayed friends with them after we divorced. But what else is a publicist supposed to do in this business?' Veronica smirked at Kirsten before placing the cigarette in the centre of her lips with only her tongue and then sparked the lighter. She took a short drag and shot the thin plume of smoke upwards like the steam from an old train.

'Was that a question for me?' Kirsten asked.

'Oh no,' Veronica smiled before taking another drag. 'Danny's the old guard of celebrity publicists darling. He wouldn't know how to operate in your world now with your phones and your instagram and pant suits. I don't think he's done anything in a while. Never did quite get on his feet again after we left L.A. More so after we got divorced. I don't think he knows how to function in this business without me. Never has. Drops my name to get a meeting here and there. Probably why he's calling.'

'Surely he doesn't really need to work now?'

'I don't know darling. I couldn't tell you what that man's finances were like even when I was married to him. But I do know he's been out of the game too long. He's never going to be able to find the next big thing again.'

'Like you.'

'Like me, darling. You gotta have a nose for it. You gotta be able to see something other people can't. And he could. For a time there he really could.'

'Until he couldn't.'

'Well, yes. You only get a few bombs until you're poison. Until it becomes not just a coincidence.'

'Maybe it's just age,' Kirsten said softly, mumbling to herself.

Veronica scoffed and let the smoke she had just inhaled curl and linger around her face instead of blowing it up and away like she had done several times before. She raised a singular eyebrow high up her forehead.

'It's taste,' she said flatly. Kirsten nodded, still unconvinced but not still interested in starting an argument. 'If it was age,' Veronica continued, 'then what were all those people doing in the crowd last night? He and I are the same age. And here I am.'

'Men. It was mostly men last night.'

'People, whatever. For the record, I definitely saw a few women in the crowd. And what about the stage door when we were leaving? Those people waiting for autographs. I saw some women there.'

'Friends maybe. Gay men, who have friends, who are women.'

Veronica sat up and spun around on her chair to face Kirsten. 'Darling what is this?' she asked before taking another drag and waving her hand up and down in the space between them.

'What is what?'

'This thing about everyone last night being gay?'

'It's not a thing.'

'It certainly seems like one.'

'It's important to know these things. To know who your audience is.'

'Well I told you who it was.'

'But I'm telling you who it is *now*.'

Veronica's head dipped towards the desk. She folded one arm across in front of her and stared at the smouldering, curling smoke emanating from between her fingers in her upturned palm. Kirsten watched her, tense and coiled in the process of digesting the information and allowed her a few moments of silence alone with it before commenting again. 'There's nothing wrong with having a mostly gay fan base, Veronica,' she said gently. 'It's just something to be aware of. It's smart business.'

'Just because there is a large group of older men coming to see a one woman show in a theatre in the city, doesn't mean they're all gay.' Kirsten coughed, trying her hardest to keep the sip of coffee she just took from splattering over the chair in front of her.

'Anyway, even if that were true, I don't see my audience like that.' Veronica said scrunching her nose up.

'Like what?'

'Like, that!'

'As gays?'

'They're just people.'

'Well that's good,' Kirsten mumbled before burying herself into her laptop again, trying to ignore the increasingly burning glare she was on the receiving end of. 'You can say gay though. It's ok.'

'Well darling we never even had that word for it before. It didn't matter. These men were just,' she trailed off and pressed two fingers hard against her forehead. 'I don't know, they were just *friendly*. They were the ones that were always escorting you in and out of parties, holding your purse or chatting to the people beside you at dull dinner tables. That's all. Why do you have to label everything like that?'

She was no longer making eye contact but fidgeted aggressively with the objects on the vanity beneath her again. Kirsten sighed heavily, but managed to avoid it making obnoxious. 'So how long was Danny your publicist for anyway?' she asked, hoping the terrible segue worked. She heard the rustle of Veronica's dress and looked up to see her leaning over to stub out her cigarette before standing up and walking over to the half box of mirrors in the corner.

'Fifteen years,' she replied, sighing. 'We were married for twelve of them.'

'And how was that?'

'Hell,' she said quickly, sitting herself back down. 'Remind me again what Amy wanted?'

'Who?'

Veronica let out another exasperated sigh. 'Amy darling, my daughter. You said she called as well. What did she want?'

'She didn't say. Just that she would try you again.'

'Strange,' Veronica said folding her arms. 'They must have spoken to each other beforehand. Something must be up. I can smell the faint scent of a favour lingering.'

'They don't usually call for anything else?'

'Those two? No.'

'Do they get along?'

'At times,' Veronica said, standing up again and starting to pull at the sides of her dress in the mirror. 'When one needs money and the other needs attention. It always seems to oscillate back and forth though as to who needs what.' She wandered over to a clothing rack stacked with long black dress bags and began fingering their hangers gently. 'And when they can't figure that out,' she said, pulling a bag out and holding it up. 'They come to me.'

'I read Amy's interview in Vanity Fair. About that film she has coming out in the summer. It was a nice write up,' Kirsten said quietly. 'Did you see it?'

Veronica turned and smiled at Kirsten but it was strained. It stretched her lips wide and thin and didn't crease her eyes at all. It was a smile of acknowledgement only. 'Yes, of course,' she said. 'So nice.'

Silently, she laid the black dress bag on the other end of the couch that Kirsten was perched on and gently pulled down on the tiny zipper at the front. Reaching inside with one hand, she pulled out a mass of black, shimmering sequins that when free of the cheap polyester casing of the bag, tumbled gently to the floor, gathering in soft, undulating folds around her feet. When she pinched the hanger between her fingers and angled it slightly higher to allow it to take its shape once again, it unraveled itself to become a floor length ball gown with thin shoulder straps, a deep, sweeping boat neck and a thick mermaid tail plume at its base. The bulbs from the mirror over the vanity quickly sent reflections of the shimmering discs in the fabric ricocheting around the room dancing and twirling as she moved and examined the dress more closely.

'Darling check for the reviews again would you?' she asked finally, placing the dress down gently against the couch again and standing back with her arms folded. Flecks of light twinkled across her face and neck and she leant forward peering into the fabric. 'They can't still not be up, surely,' Veronica said.

'One second,' Kirsten mumbled, tapping away at her keyboard and squinting into the screen. 'No, still nothing I'm sorry,' she winced.

'Is this how things are now?' Veronica trailed off, mumbling before turning around, her arms folded tightly across her chest. 'You know back in the day, reviews were published *that* bloody night. Critics were like piranhas, munching at each other like mad to get their words seen first. Now, what is it? Spellcheck and autocorrect and they still can't turn anything in on time.'

'It could be a good sign,' Kirsten said softly. 'Let's wait and see.'

'I should think so. Christ...' Veronica rolled her eyes and returned to the clothes hanger. She tapped her long nails over her bicep and edged closer to Kirsten. Her breathing grew heavier and she began twitching her feet inside her heels. 'Fine. Well, let's go over last night then. Do you have your notes? You said you took some.'

Kirsten turned and dove into her handbag, emerging with a small black Moleskine, which she flicked open several pages in and scanned down with her index finger. 'So I think I mentioned to you before, that you seemed to get quite a lot of feedback, response, or whatever you want to call it, on the story you opened with. The one about your fling with Al Pacino.'

'Ah,' Veronica said smiling, looking to the ceiling and closing her eyes briefly. 'Yes, I remember.'

'Yeah, there was quite a lot of noise which was good. People liked it. There was some pretty loud shouting even.' Veronica nodded along, still deep in her reminiscing of the moment.

'At the time too,' she said softly, smirking to herself.

'So I thought maybe, we should try easing into it? Y'know, like not open so heavy. Keep the good stuff for when you're a bit further in?'

'Darling it's all good.'

Kirsten laughed awkwardly. 'You wanna keep people engaged though. Having sex with Al Pacino in your trailer on set in Turkey is spicy. Let the dust settle and then tell it maybe?'

'I never said we had sex,' Veronica said, unfolding her arms and picking up the black dress again, holding it out in front of her.

'Well,' Kirsten said looking up. 'However you want to paint it.'

'I don't want any trouble. It's the problem with telling stories about people who aren't dead yet. Also he was married at the time. '

'You were too weren't you?'

'Barely.'

Kirsten waited briefly before continuing on as she was certain Veronica was going to elaborate. To fall into some deep stream of consciousness about the twilight of her marriage but instead she simply leant forward and slowly picked up the dress again to glare silently at it, totally distracted and by its glow. She returned to her notes, scanning the pages for the next thing to say and as she looked up again, she saw Veronica had positioned herself in front of the tall mirrors in the corner. The bright discs tripled in quantity as they bounced off one mirror onto the next, into the vortex and then back onto the wall. She swayed gently to and fro with it, waltzing as she pressed it against her.

'They seemed to like the bit about the Golden Globes after party,' Kirstens said interrupting Veronica's daydreaming. 'The one with Jerry Hall and Liza Minelli. Big claps again, cheering, etc. Mostly when you mentioned Liza.'

Veronica turned and smiled, the dress still pressed tightly against her. 'Good,' she said quietly and spun back around.

'Got anymore Liza stories, maybe?'

'What do you mean?'

'Like is there anything else you could say about her?'

'Well I'm sure I could pull something out of somewhere. Who hasn't got a Liza Minelli story in this business,' she said.'But really?'

'I mean, again just gauging from their response, it might be a good idea.' Veronica sighed and rubbed her temples aggressively. 'Didn't you tell me once something funny about her at a charity benefit?'

'Maybe, I can't remember…'

'Something about her trying to find cocaine and then someone throwing it to her from the audience as she was singing?'

'Probably, I don't know darling. I can't remember. I'd really rather not go on about her. Truly. It's just a bit, I don't know. She's just…' Veronica shook her head as she trailed off.

'But if people want to hear it,' Kirsten said glaring down at her notes again. 'And judging by their reactions, it seems like they do, I think you should consider telling it. Goes back to what we were discussing before.'

'Your theory about everyone being a homosexual?'

'About knowing your audience.'

'So are they writing this, or am I?'

'There's no reason why this has to be locked down.'

'And if people come a second time, what if they notice it's a different show? How would that look?'

'Is that a bad thing?'

'Darling, I adore Liza, but she's just y'know,' Veronica winced into the mirror and then turned around again. 'So damn camp. It's hard to take anyone seriously who is actually that camp.'

Kirsten eyed up the woman stood before her; her tight black dress that she had been in since the morning, her sky high, patent leather stilettos and stacked brunette wigs, the countless clusters of sequins from the accessories of the costumes that dangled around her, the dense fake lashes that weighed down her eyes, the long, red, acrylic nails that extended out from her slender fingers, her face that was pulled and pinched and pinned and pricked, her overdrawn lips and razor thin eyebrows and her filled cheekbones, her glowing vanity with its excessive collection of perfumes, cigarettes, powder pink compacts, framed glamour shots of herself in heavy silver outlines, forests of make-up pencils and brushes and then finally back up to her and mumbled quietly to herself. 'Sure,' she said.

'What?' Veronica spat, turning only her head to face Kirsten, leaving the rest of her body facing towards the mirror still.

'Whatever you think' Kirsten managed to get out, clearing her throat at the same time as she flicked through her notebook.

'And also darling you have to remember what this is. It's an autobiography. It's not some tabloid slag fest. I'm not going to stand up there gossiping for ninety minutes. I want it to be aspirational.'

'You mean inspirational?'

'That's what I said. It's not about giving people tidbits of old Hollywood hearsay. It's about a young Australian woman, going out into the world, working her ass off and succeeding. It's about navigating and dodging all that dick swinging, old boys club, studio bullshit and coming out on top. That's what I want from this show. For other women to see it and feel inspired to follow their dreams. See, you say there were mostly men in the audience last night darling, but I think it might be a good thing.'

'How so?'

'Those men will go home to their wives or girlfriends,' she said as she spun around and flung the dress against the couch before pacing towards Kirsten, 'and say, You know what I saw tonight, honey? I saw an actress, on the other side of seventy, up there on stage, bright and accomplished and thriving and this is how she did it.'

'Wives and girlfriends?'

'Yes. And daughters. Children are the future, and all that.' she waved her hand in the air, trailing off completely.

'Right.'

'They won't ever have to hustle like I hustled though.'

'But that's the point right?' Kirsten asked.

'Yes. Standing on the shoulders of giants,' she said as she leant over her vanity again, lifted the lid of the silver box, produced another cigarette and plucked the lighter from beside it. 'What else did you write down in that little book of yours?'

Kirsten flicked forward several pages, all of which were madly covered with notes scribbled in smudged black ink. She looked up to Veronica for a moment and sighed. 'I think we need to talk about the film.'

'What film?'

Kirsten was silent, but pursed her lips and sighed in a way that Veronica was able to read almost instantly. 'No,' she said at her, before turning to take another drag. 'Why?'

'I just think that-'

'What for?' she snapped.

'If you let me talk first?'

'Fine.'

Kirsten paused and took a deep inhale. 'There are some comments on twitter that I saw from people in the audience about it.'

'Comments like what?'

'Just people saying that it seems like a bit of an obvious gap in the story of the show. Your story.'

'Yes that's very intentional.'

'I understand, but…' Kirsten trailed off, letting out the chest full of air she had sucked in before. 'I think a lot of people came, expecting you to discuss it. Or at least mention it.'

'Well I'm sorry but, I don't know what to tell them?' Veronica shrugged, blowing out smoke. 'Who even cares about it anymore. It was all so long ago now.'

'I think a lot of people still do.'

'Yes your gays would. Shockingly.'

'And what's wrong with that?'

'Absolutely not.'

'Why?'

'Because it's cheap Kirsten. It's a cheap, kitschy laugh for them. And it undermines the whole concept of what I just told you I wanted the show to be.'

'But don't you see it more like having the platform to set the record straight? Years of the story of this film and what it did to you, being told behind your back by gossip columnists, by the director and the producers, biographers even. And now you have a captive audience all to yourself and you don't want to mention it?'

Veronica took a long drag of her cigarette and squinted at her silently. 'Why are you suggesting these changes when you know we already have something good? The show sold out.'

Kirsten shrugged slightly and quickly went back to flicking through her notes. Veronica glared at her curiously for a moment longer before turning back to her vanity. 'The answer is no.' Kirsten didn't respond, only letting her shoulders sink slightly down towards the ground. I will not pander to people's sick interest in that terrible film or what it did to my life,' Veronica said firmly. 'I won't do it.'

Kirsten looked briefly up at Veronica who hadn't turned back to face her. She was looking down at the dress as it cascaded past her lower half and collected delicately on the floor. 'Anything else?' she asked, sounding slightly bored.

'No, nothing. That was it.'

Veronica shot her a strained, passive aggressive smile and turned back to the mirrors. 'Christ I really wish those reviews would hurry up. Like they matter with a sell out show though, right? I don't know why I'm so nervous about them.'

Kirsten tried to smile hard. 'I mean, truly what does a review matter if the show is a success?' Veronica continued. 'If people are entertained. If they are there and watching and enjoying themselves, what in the hell is the purpose of a critic anyway in the face of something that is popular regardless?'

'Well there's usually a bit of a distinction between critical success and commercial success I guess?'

'Maybe in the past yes, but not now.'

'The dream is to charm the people as well as the institutions. You don't want to be seen as a sell out.'

'But what's an Academy Award worth if people aren't seeing you perform? You want to be that artist that has a shelf full of accolades but can't eat? No thank you. Not me darling. These things, they're just trinkets to me. Never cared for them. I want people to see what I do and that's all. I don't care for awards.'

'But you remembered to bring yours again, right?'

'Of course darling,' Veronica said, smugly, diving into her black handbag and producing an Oscar statuette. 'They liked this, didn't they?'

Kirsten nodded gently. She watched on as Veronica cradled the thing with both hands, pulling it closer into her chest as she did. She stopped short of totally pressing it against herself, but Kirsten was certain she would have if she weren't there watching her. She was certain that, despite her proclamations about her indifference, that in these solitary moments, she held it with the same amount of care and obsession that new mother would, sat in bed after her labor. She had seen passing glimpses of it before when Veronica had, seemingly for no reason at all, carried it with her to meetings, dinners and events that they had attended together. It would sit in anyone of her large handbags, wrapped in a piece of black velvet cloth, obscured but still visible for anyone willing to notice. It was a priceless, irreplaceable thing. Years of sweat and heartache, failure and astounding success all captured in a tiny, heavy piece of gold plated bronze.

Kirsten's phone vibrated loudly against the cushions of the couch, once and then twice quickly again. Instantly Veronica spun around and her eyes fixed down on it. For a moment Kirsten found herself staring at Veronica staring at her phone like some large cat standing over an injured bird, before she realised it was her prompt to check it. Her eye's darted up to meet hers and then quickly back down to the phone again. 'Well?' she spat. 'Anything?'

When Kirsten finally flicked it open, looking back up at her from the screen was a slightly out of focus, poorly angled, but still wholly discernible shot of an incredibly tall drag queen on Veronica's Instagram feed. She appeared to be crouching in the doorway of a small, messy kitchen with a mass of beautifully constructed brown hair all but scraping the ceiling above her. She had broad strokes of black eyeliner that flicked out from the edges of her eyes and up to her temples with enormous, feathery lashes that hung heavily over each of her eye lids and thick, overly painted lips. She stood with one hand on her hip and the other with her palm upturned to the roof and a cigarette dangling in between her fingers; the exact way she has seen Veronica do it so many times before.

Kirsten glanced up at Veronica who was now edging closer, the longer she took to respond with some sort of acknowledgement of the notification. The closer Veronica got, the more obvious it became, that the dress drag queen in the picture was in, was an exact replica of the one Veronica had been holding against her and the one she had been in on stage the night before. Kirsten peered deeper into the screen and mouthed the words that were jotted beneath the image as she scanned them. *Seeing my IDOL tonight @Veronica.Lange*

'Well?' Veronica shouted again, before lunging at the phone with one arm. Kirsten managed to pull it just out of reach in time, slamming it against her chest. 'Tell me!' she screamed. 'Is it a review? Christ.'

'It's just a notification from your Instagram, it's not a review.'

'Oh for god-sake,' she sighed, turning away. 'Fine. Well what is it then?'

'Just ah…' Kirsten glanced down at her phone again, but before she could speak, a long, skeletal hand flashed quickly across the air under her face, collecting the phone with it. She looked up to see Veronica clutching it tightly, pressing it closely to her own face.

As she squinted into the screen, the muscles around her eyes and mouth all appeared to tense together at once. Her lips pressed hard against her cheeks and her eyes widened. She did not move for some time, frozen in the strained expression examining the image that she clearly recognised but did not want to. Finally, and without saying a word, she slowly handed the phone back to Kirsten and walked off, pausing only once she arrived at the black sequinned dress again laying neatly on the end of the couch.

'Well,' she said quietly as she began holding the fabric gently between her fingers again. Kirsten felt her stomach churn slightly.

'She's clearly a big fan.'

Veronica cleared her throat in a way that was something in between a cough and growl, not making any eye contact and trying hard to appear busy.

'Have you ever even been to a drag show before?'

'Oh of course I've not been to a bloody drag show Kirsten. Honestly.'

'You should be flattered then.'

'Should I?' Veronica shouted, sarcastically. 'Really?'

'Yes,' Kirsten shot back.

A tense, silence grew between them that Kirsten felt she could have easily and quickly pushed through but still didn't. She just watched Veronica turn away, sighing, shaking her head. 'Where are those bloody reviews?' she mumbled through the screeching of wire hangers against the bar of the rack.

'I'll take the tag on the picture down then so it doesn't appear in your account,' Kirsten sighed, looking back to her phone. 'If that's what you want?' Veronica looked over blankly at her, squinted and then continued to fuss with the clothes, saying nothing. 'Just to let you know also, a few people seem to be tagging you in Amy's Vanity Fair interview also,' Kirsten said quietly.

'Why?' Veronica asked, still not making eye contact.

'Well the journalist asks her about you in the interview.'

'What does it say?'

'Didn't you say you read it?'

'I must have skipped that bit,' Veronica waved her hand dismissively.

'One second, I'll find it.' Kirsten hunched further over her phone and began scrolling and tapping manically before leaning back again. 'Your mother, Veronica Lange, wasn't there the night you won your own Academy Award. As a Best Actress winner herself, did she have any advice for you going into the ceremony or for life afterwards?'

Kirsten looked up briefly and found Veronica hovering over her.

'Do you want to hear her answer?'

'No. I don't care.'

'Why not?'

'Because the answer is no. That's the truth. If she's said anything different then she's lying. And that's on her.'

'Did she call you to tell you when she was nominated?'

'No, I found out on Entertainment Tonight like everyone else did.'

'But you watched it? The ceremony?'

'Some of it, yes,' she said in a deeper voice than usual. 'Her father was there that night. In the crowd. He walked her in on that red carpet as well. Smiling, beaming like the idiot he is. Christ knows why or how he managed to wrangle it with her to go. I didn't even know they were speaking at the time. He wasn't around in the beginning. Never there when she needed babysitting or help with school or singing lessons or anything like that. But, she starts to do well on her own, in this business, his business, gets this nomination and suddenly she's the apple of his eye. And she eats it up. It's pathetic really.'

'And you two haven't spoken since?'

'Who, Amy?'

'Yes.'

'No, we talk. I mean, she calls. She calls to check in on me the way a nurse would peek through a curtain to see if a patient was still breathing. She calls to talk *at* me. Not with me. But y'know, she kept things warm enough between us for long enough to get where she is today. The name Amy Shields with the addendum *daughter of Veronica Lange,* has done a great deal for that girl but do you think she shows an ounce of appreciation for it? Of recognising the work that went in before her? No. I had no one. I had a mother who was a housewife and a father who ran a pharmacy. What did they know about show business? Nothing. She got it all handed to her on a plate, took it and walked off without saying a word.'

'I wonder what she was calling for then?'

'Let's wait and see.'

Veronica bent slightly at her waist to collect the dress again from the couch but stopped half way down when something on the vanity seemed to catch her eye. 'What's all that?' she asked, gesturing to a small pile of letters and documents, bound together in a brown rubber band.

Kirsten looked up slowly. 'Oh, from front of house. They said some stuff came for you this morning. I didn't look at it yet.' She shrugged mindlessly and went back to fussing on her phone, leaving Veronica to leaf through the pile in silence.

Her long fingers tore at the edges of pamphlets and plastic packets, scanning the contents and then eventually scrunching up into loose balls whatever she found uninteresting. She came finally to a small postcard sized envelope in a pale, powder pink colour which also happened to be the only handwritten one in the collection. She held it up and squinted into the curly, flamboyant ink and pulled it back again smiling. There was no address or postage stamp and simply had *Dear Ms Lange* written elegantly across it. 'I wonder what this could be?' she said, out into the room to no one in particular. With more care and attention than she had given the rest of the pile combined and using the edge of her long red nail to slice the top of the packet, she slid out a sheet of card the precise colour and dimensions of the envelope. Kirsten looked up and squinted towards the thing she held pinched between both her hands. Even from the couch she could see make out the flashy writing on both sides as Veronica twisted it back and forth, her smile growing wider as she did. 'I think it's fan mail.'

'Who's it from?' Kirsten asked.

'I have no idea. Hand me my glasses darling, they're beside you.'

She held the card at arms length, raising it up and down, focusing first and then clearing her throat. 'Dear Ms Lange,' she began, still smiling. 'Please first excuse my handwriting, I have been told many times now it has a certain flair that makes it hard to read. We wanted to express our gratitude to you for bringing this show to life. It's such an honest and open piece of art. We have been huge fans of yours since before we care to remember and still have memories of lining up to see you in *Goodbye Istanbul* as nervous teenagers together, many moons ago. You are a vision and we eagerly await your next project as we have always. Sincerely, Lance and Jules.'

Veronica put the card down and smiled broadly at Kirsten. 'God, isn't that so sweet? High school sweethearts lining up to see my movie all those years ago. And still together all this time later.'

'It's very cute.'

'You know I've actually had quite a few men come up to me and tell me over the years that they've proposed to their wives to that film? At drive-ins or after the cinema. There must just be something about it. You know I feel sorry for your generation sometimes darling, these films they belch into the world now. The films we used to make, had a lasting kind of power. Impact,' she said shaking the card in the air. Kirsten nodded slowly, looking at the letter and then back at Veronica, her smile turning to a grimace.

'Veronica that letter is clearly from two guys, not a husband and wife,' Kirsten said.

'What?'

'The couple who wrote you that letter…'

'Yes?'

'They're a gay couple.'

'Oh Christ, here we go.' Veronica shouted, flapping her arms about. 'Well darling, it says here, very clearly,' she said, pushing the card towards Kirsten, 'Lance and Jules. *Jules*.' She tapped the bottom of the card with her fingernail inches from Kirsten's face.

'It's probably Julian,' Kirsten said flatly.

'What man gets around being called Jules?'

Kirsten shrugged. 'I know a guy called Jules.'

'Yes I imagine you would. But this is Julia or Julie or Juliette or something.'

Kirsten stayed silent while she sat glaring at Veronica. She felt one of her eyebrows rising slowly in disbelief like the mercury of a hot thermometer. She watched as Veronica's posture straightened, her shoulders pinned back and her nose tilted slightly upwards towards the ceiling.

'I don't know why you insist on pushing this? Still. Again,' Veronica said, sighing loudly.

'I'm not trying to make this an issue. I just don't know why you find it so offensive to be adored by gay men.'

'It's not offensive to me. I don't find it offensive.'

'Well then what's all this?'

'What?'

'This!' Kirsten gestured to Veronica holding the letter out between her finger and thumb now like a rogue hair she had just found in a plate of food. Veronica looked at it herself and immediately let it drop to the table, pressing her face into her hands moaning. Slowly she stood up and wandered over to one of the clothes rack and placed both hands gently on the rail, bracing herself. She hung her head low letting her hair fall around her neck, closed her eyes and took in a deep, slow breath.

'How do you expect me to know how this is supposed to work?' she said softly, raising her head and opening her eyes again, but only to face the wall in front of her.

'How what is supposed to work?'

'This,' she said gesturing to Kirsten's phone. 'All this. And them. These men.'

'I don't think I know what you mean?'

'What am I supposed to do with this information?'

Kirsten was silent again, scrunching her lips tightly together. 'I don't think they expect you to do anything. Just what you have been doing. They seem to have gathered around you on their own steam.'

'Oh really? And why's that you think?'

'Why do I think gays latch themselves on to famous women?'

'Yes.'

'I think if we had the answer to that question, we'd be very rich by now.'

'And so this is a money thing then?'

'Isn't everything in this?'

Veronica sighed heavily and turned finally to face her. 'For the record, I've seen how this plays out,' she said through a long breath. 'We all have, haven't we?'

Kirsten shrugged nonchalantly to indicate she was most likely an exception to Veronica's generalisation. 'Once the sex has gone, once you've crossed that threshold of being something to bed, and you become purely ornamental to the people whose attention you used to hold for other reasons, you become something only to be admired, from afar. Something glossy and sparkling, like a twirling ballerina in a cheap jewellery box. Then the men go. And then once the women realise there is now one less competitor in the ring for them, they go too. And what's left?' She glared at Kirsten with her eyes wide. 'Hmm?'

'I don't know.'

'The gays. This is what we are left with. Women like me. In this,' she said gesturing around her.

'I think it's probably a little deeper than that.'

'Is it?'

'Yes.'

'What if I don't want gay fans?'

'I would probably keep that thought to yourself.'

'But truly, what if I just came right out and said thank you, that's very kind, but no thanks.'

'Why would you want to do that?'

'Because I'm not *ready*,' Veronica said sighing, appearing like she may soon be on the brink of tears. Her throat sounded full and she mumbled the last word, before clearing her throat again. 'Darling, I'm just not ready for that yet.'

'Ok,' Kirsten said quietly, edging closer, preparing herself to have to possibly console her.

'And why is it even an inevitability?'

'I don't think having gay fans is something that's inevitable.'

'No, I don't mean that specifically. I mean just this big descent into the camp and the kitsch for women? Why is it something I even need to be *ready* for? Like it's menopause or something?'

'I think everything probably becomes a little camp after a while, doesn't it? Once something becomes unfashionable. Clothes, films, songs. I don't think it's just about women in show business.'

'I think women suffer from it the most. Who suffers when a pair of shoes goes out of fashion?'

'Why can't you see this as something to leverage though? To use to your advantage?'

'Why would I want to undo a lifetime of work of trying to be taken seriously, only to be turned in to some chintzy doll?'

'Well because you just said a moment ago that critical praise doesn't concern you.'

Veronica pursed her lips together tightly and folded her arms. 'It's not the same thing.'

'Isn't it? Then why didn't you just go with the Tennessee Williams shit then? At least it has substance?'

'Oh and what I'm doing now doesn't?'

'I didn't mean that. I mean't if you are so concerned about being labelled as a camp icon. Though I don't know what's not camp about Tennessee Williams.'

'See! Why?' Kirsten shrugged as Veronica shouted. 'I am not, for a second, saying I don't appreciate it. I don't know who is sat out there in the dark, I don't care. But these kinds of fans,' she said, bolting to the bench of her vanity and holding up the purple card again. 'These kinds of calm, distanced but still adoring fans, are the ones I covet. Long lasting, classy, minimal baggage. If they're straight then who cares. Like I said, I don't see it.'

Kirsten looked up again and leaned forward, squinting into the card. 'These sorts of fans,' Veronica continued shouting, shaking the card in the air. 'Measured adoration. Long term adoration. Controlled fandom. Not this firecracker of camp, glittery, hysterical obsession from the gays, soaring fast and high into the sky only to explode into a billion pieces once it burns itself out and rain its fire down on you. No darling not for me. No thank you. I will stick to the men falling in love with their soul mates in the theatre thank you.'

Veronica tossed the purple card towards Kirsten where it twirled, briefly airborne in the space between them, before landing delicately on one of the cushions on the couch. Kirsten glared at it, disinterested for a moment, then examining the side Veronica had just read and then the back. 'I think you missed a bit.'

Veronica placed both hands on her hips and pulled her shoulders back. 'Ok, well?' she asked shrugging. Kirsten cleared her throat and held it out to adjust her eyes. 'Please find enclosed this polaroid of us,' she said loudly. 'With one of our gorgeous King Charles Cavalier Spaniels. We named her Veronica after you.'

Veronica leant over to the bench where the Polaroid had been laying face down, flicked it over and glared with her eyes wide and intense down into the tight, white frame of two well dressed men, both on the better side of sixty, cradling a very young puppy. She collapsed into the chair, holding her face and sighed heavily. 'Oh for Christ-sake,' she groaned.

The heavy, metallic reverberation of Kirsten's phone humming into the fabric of the couch again punctuated the silence in the room that followed. Kirsten didn't move at first to grab it, waiting instead for a reaction from Veronica, which after the second hum brought her piercing glare down upon it. Kirsten reached over to it and held it tightly before swiping it open. Veronica bolted up from the chair, her eyes wide, her arms folded and her body frozen. 'One second,' she said quietly, anticipating the prompt from Veronica already to hurry up. She swiped at her screen in silence, peering closer into the glow. 'Oh good…'

'What? What is it?'

'A review.'

'Finally! Christ. Ok, let me sit down,' she said, darting around the room searching for something more comfortable to fall into. 'No wait, I think I'd rather stand. Don't start yet, let me focus.' She took a long, deep inhale, closing her eyes and relaxing her hands down besides her waist. 'Ok, I'm ready. Which one is it?'

'TimeOut.'

'Fine. Ok, give it to me,' she said extending her arm out for the phone. Kirsten went to do the same, before Veronica pulled back violently and folded her arms again. 'No, wait. I can't. You do it.'

'Do what?'

'Read it! Read it to me.'

Kirsten enlarged the screen and squinted into the light. 'Last night -'

'Wait!' Veronica screeched, raising both her hands up and hanging her head. She dashed over to the vanity, knocking over several bottles of her perfume and the other canisters of make-up and liquids as she dove into her cigarette box. She straightened up and drew in quickly. 'Ok, go.' The words were released with the exhale of smoke that she then proceeded to bat away, waving her hand back and forth. Kirsten looked up to ensure she would not be interrupted once again and then proceeded to squint into the screen before clearing her throat.

'Last night at the East Sydney Palladium, we were treated to a flamboyant power mince through one of the Golden Ages of Hollywood, with our guide being none other than Veronica Lange herself. *My Life in Pictures*, as the title suggests, is a neat and chronological look through her career in film, using a series of iconic images to which she stands there and describes, in vivid detail, the stories behind them...'

Kirsten looked up slowly. Veronica was standing with the cigarette in her mouth and her hands on her hips, inhaling short sharp breaths without taking it out her mouth again. She took a deep breath herself and continued on. 'Lange, possibly one of the most famous faces and personalities of the era, is energetic and seems comfortable in her new role as keeper of memories of this important period in time for pop culture. Her reign as one of the many queens of the silver screen was during the era that gave us

China Town, *Jaws*, *Network*, *Taxi Driver*, *Love Story* and *Midnight Express* along with introducing people like Martin Scorsese, Faye Dunaway, Meryl Streep, Al Pacino and George Lucas to the world.'

'Ok,' Veronica mumbled looking anxious.

Kirsten paused, reading ahead slightly before clearing her throat and starting again. 'But for anyone old enough to remember Lange as the actress she was back then, it's a confronting sight to see her like this. Entertaining as she is, the show is shallow as she spends almost the full 90 minutes simply recounting scandalous trysts and campy feuds with her contemporaries in graphic detail, dropping names like loose pearls from a cheap, broken necklace. It nourishes the lowest common denominator's hunger for backstage, behind the scenes, after hours gossip, but what of those that remember her in *Bridges*? In *Mrs Highsmith*? In *Goodbye Istanbul*? Details of her acting achievements are well covered as she basks in the audience's response to even passing mention of her biggest hits, however there is one gaping hole in her story that no doubt a vast chunk of her more, let's say colourful, fans had clearly come in the hopes of hearing her talk about. When will she ever mention *that* film? When will she finally talk about *Isabella*? When will Veronica Lange realise she is the only person in the world not willing to talk about the sole reason for that spectacular Hollywood career dive? A film so bad, so poorly reviewed, still to this day, that even after her two Academy Awards before it, it sent her packing back home to Australia? Take nothing away from her, Lange is a vision on stage. Glistening in Bob Mackie-esque couture, nails long and sharp, hair out and high, gesturing in wide, elegant waves of her elegant limbs. But for those of you who have come to see the actress, save your money. Lange is not acting. She seems too comfortable now only in her role as a campy caricature of her former self. And so does her new queer audience.'

Kirsten pulled her phone away from her face slowly, letting it drop in her hands to settle on her lap. Her cheeks pulsated bright and red and her eyes stung but she didn't dare look up at Veronica yet. She scrolled through a few more pages, digging desperately to see if there might be something else to distract her. When she finally relented and looked to the other side of the room, she saw Veronica standing there, swaying slightly with one arm folded across her chest and the other stuck up at a right angle, her cigarette dangling precariously between her fingers, mostly now just ash and butt. A final, dazed sway of her body sent the stack of black, charred remnants tumbling to the floor like dark snow.

'Let's wait and see what the others say before we- '

'It's fine,' Veronica said, turning and dropping the butt into the ashtray.

'I think some more will come-'

'It's fine.' She settled back into the chair facing her vanity mirror. She reached down into a small drawer beneath the bench and produced a thick, stapled script. It's pages were foxed and folded, curling up at all corners and with bright yellow tabs of Post-Its sticking out at various sections. She opened it slowly and splayed it across the space in front of her, resting her head on her hand, scanning it in total silence.

Kirsten watched Veronica from the couch, hunching over it, almost certain she wasn't even reading any of the words that looked back up at her. Her phone buzzed over and over, with more reviews that flooded through after, scanning them all, *The Guardian*, *The Sydney Times*, *The Daily Telegraph*, *HuffPost*, then every tag, every notification, barely pausing to absorb the masses of text and content, looking only for the words she knew were hurting the most. Camp. Kitsch. Irreverent. Ostentatious. And every time, there they were, more and more. Over the top. Garish. Flamboyant. She glanced up at Veronica again. She wasn't seeing them or even hearing what was currently spewing out across the internet about her, but it was obvious she was somehow feeling it. The words, like little arrows, flung into her back as she curled further and further into herself.

'Tell me what the ticket sales are,' Veronica mumbled over the pages of the script.

'I'm sorry?'

'The sales for tonight. Check them can you?' she said again, sounding slightly drunk.

Kirsten reached for her phone, but didn't open it. 'We checked them last night though. They were fine.'

'But tell me what they are now, right now. I want to know. Tell me the numbers again.'

Kirsten watched Veronica for a moment longer before bowing into her phone again and waiting as the page loaded before her, glaring into the sea of the hundreds of tiny squares indicating the individual seats and their numbers as they curved around in the arc of the theatre floor plan. She sighed as it continued to refresh, rubbing the back of her neck, allowing her eyes to adjust to the tiny, compressed text and images of the page. But once it stopped, she pulled the phone right into her face, squinting hard, enlarging the screen with her fingers again and again. She let it rest against her lap, before shoving it back under her eyes.

The squares that should have been, and were only just the night before, all red; red for booked, for confirmed, for paid and reserved, instead were now simply white. Rows and rows of blank, empty cells glowing hot and bright on her phone, burning up at her as she bore back down onto them. Even with only a superficial count, racing her eyes around the screen, she could see barely twenty confirmed. Twenty five at most. Twenty-five red and booked squares in a theatre for over a thousand people. 'I ah,' Kirsten mumbled nervously, counting them over and over, trying each time with desperate precision to find another one with each attempt. Finally, she looked up at Veronica who she saw was now looking into the ceiling, but with one curious eye firmly locked on her. Kirsten felt her hand impulsively cover the screen before she placed it down on her lap. 'Shit.'

The reaction fell out her mouth before she even had a chance to think about how to respond appropriately. 'What? Veronica spat back at her quickly. Kirsten remained silent, glaring into the screen. 'Shit, what?' Veronica said again louder.

'I ah,' Kirsten mumbled diving back into the screen again. 'One second…'

'Kirsten what? Bloody tell me. Did we sell out again? Is it all gone?'

'No.'

'Ok, then what? What is it at?'

She refreshed the screen once again and then sighed. 'I think there's a problem.'

One of Veronica's eye brows lifted slowly and her lips pressed tightly together, which seemed reason enough for Kirsten to elaborate without being asked. 'There seems to only be about twenty-five seats booked. I don't know why though. I am just trying to che-'

'Twenty five?' Veronica snapped.

'For tonight's show,' Kirsten said slowly. 'Twenty-five tickets.'

'I'm sorry, what?' Veronica scoffed with a devastated, light laughter. 'That's impossible. Check again. Check it now.'

Kirsten was silent. All she could manage to do was shrink herself back into the couch, flicking her fingers across the glass of the phone helplessly as the sea of tiny squares loaded and reloaded again, still with the same, meagre amount of red dots appearing each time.

'And?' Veronica's voice grew shrill.

'I don't know what's going on,' Kirsten said finally making eye contact.

'There has to be some mistake. You checked it last night. You showed me. It was nearly sold out again. This is impossible. Check it again!'

Kirsten stood up quickly and headed to the opposite corner of the tiny room. 'Let me make a call.'

'Yes,' Veronica said sharply. 'Do that. Make your calls.' She waved to her and collapsed further into her chair. 'Go.'

Veronica's shoulder's fell towards the bench of the vanity. Her head dipped, and her hair fell loosely down around her face as she planted both hands over her eyes, shaking her head. 'Twenty-five?' she mumbled, with her voice almost totally muffled by her palms. 'Impossible.'

She rose from the chair and stood facing Kirsten who was huddled now, deep into the corner of the room, whispering into her phone. Veronica folded her arms and paced gently towards her stopping just as she appeared to click the call shut and then slowly turned to face her.

'The theatre offers people the ability to sell the tickets back to them so they can re-sell it on if they can't come to a show. It's kind of a way to stop scalpers price gouging I guess.'

'And?' Veronica spat back.

'We did know that.'

'So what?'

'Well, there appears to have been some cancellations.'

'*Some*?' Veronica screamed. '*Some*? That theatre holds over a thousand people darling. *Some* is five. *Some* is a dozen...'

'We had at least two thirds sold when I checked last night. I showed you.'

'So what fucking happened then?' Veronica stood staring down at Kirsten as she crouched over her phone, breathing slowly through her nose. 'A bad TimeOut review has that much sway on people's opinions these days? I won't believe it.'

'No, but it doesn't help.'

Veronica scoffed so loudly, it made her body convulse forward as if she had just coughed up a fishbone. 'No,' she said, 'No it doesn't. Twenty-five tickets, I mean...'

She turned to walk back towards the space in between the mirrors, one hand on her hip and the other pressing against her forehead. She paced back and forth to her vanity twice and then a third time before storming over to Kirsten to stand over her.

'And what about tomorrow?'

'What do you mean?'

'The tickets for tomorrow. Check them.'

'Now?'

'Yes bloody now!'

Kirsten held her phone up again and flicked across it quickly before mumbling, 'Thirty.'

'My god,' she howled. 'And the night after?'

'Twenty-two.'

'And next week?'

Kirsten stayed silent this time. She just looked up at Veronica and sighed gently. Veronica turned towards the mirrors once more and collapsed heavily into her chair. Her sharp elbows slapping the table as she pressed her face into her palms and laughed manically. 'Twenty five,' she growled through her fingers. 'Twenty. Five. How?'

'Veronica I don't know…'

'And what of their applause last night? What was that for, if not for me?' she said releasing her face and leaning into the glass. 'Where did that go? Kirsten where did that go? Tell me.'

She glared into Veronica's face blankly with nothing to offer back but the silent acknowledgment that she was listening.

'And all the press we did before?' Veronica continued. 'What of that? Just shouting into the wind was it?'

'We didn't do any press. You didn't want to.'

'The posters. The bloody posters Kirsten.'

'You wanted to keep it discreet, remember?'

'Yes but the posters.'

'Well I mean…'

'Where are they?'

'We put them up Veronica, like you asked, but…'

'But then what? What's happened in the last twenty four hours then? Tell me?'

'We still have some time for tonight.'

'Time for what?'

'People showing up late. Last minute sales.'

'Oh Kirsten for Christ sake, don't be so ridiculous. This isn't fucking *Hamilton*.' She leant back, exposing her now red and distressed face to the ceiling. 'Who are these people showing up?'

'People who might not have been able to get tickets last night?'

'Yes the same people reading all those reviews I imagine.'

Veronica leant forward again and turned her body to face the wall, with one eye fixed on Kirsten. She inhaled slowly and fell deeper into the chair. 'What else are people saying on that thing?' she asked flicking her hand towards her phone.

'On what?'

'On whatever,' she growled. 'Just tell me.'

Kirsten anxiously flicked open her phone. 'I guess kinda similar stuff really to the reviews.'

'Right. So, that the show is camp? That it's kitzche and ostentatious. That I'm washed up...' she said trailing off.

'There's less of a nasty tone to it though from the people, than the critics.'

'Oh ok, so they're calling it ostentatious but then putting a smiley face or something at the end of it?'

'I mean, yes they're saying this stuff, but it's not necessarily a bad thing.'

'Oh sweetheart, c'mon. Really? This is your gays again is it? This is how their love is shown? I won't go on that stage and perform to twenty-five people. I can't,' Veronica said shaking her face. 'I won't do it.'

As she started to pace again between the mirrors, even from her position in the couch, Kirsten could see she was grinding her teeth. 'How could you expect me to do that? After last night?'

'I get it Veronica, I understand. We need to fix it.'

'*We*?' Veronica cackled, throwing her head back so almost every molar in her mouth was briefly exposed. 'Oh honey. Tell me how you didn't know things were this bad only until now?'

'You saw me check it with you just then.'

'Tell me that stupid phone of yours doesn't go ping every time someone cancels a ticket?'

'It doesn't.'

'I don't believe it. You want me to go out there regardless.'

'No one wants that.'

'... no matter who is sat out there in the dark. No matter if it's just one gaping black void facing back at me as I stand there alone, doing that monkey dance there under those lights, that's all you need, right? That's all anyone needs.' She fell dramatically against the table, crumpling herself up with her arms wrapped tightly around her head and her shoulders curved up around her neck as she lay her face against the table.

'I might have an idea,' Kirsten said sighing.

'What is your idea?' Veronica asked, only partly audible through her folded limbs and fallen hall.

'What if we got someone in to talk to you and filmed it also?'

Veronica lifted her head and squinted into the mirror towards her. 'Who, like Vanity Fair?'

'Not quite.'

'Then who?' she said shrugging before going to lay her head down once more.

'Like someone from that crowd last night. To come in, here. And we could record them talking to you talking about the show. Take some pictures. Ask them to post it. One of these guys has to live nearby, I'm sure they would jump at the chance to do that.'

'What?' Veronica asked sarcastically. 'Like an interview? From a punter? Are you joking? Kirsten darling, I mean really...'

'No just like a chat. And I'm talking about the people giving you that standing ovation last night, Veronica. Them.'

She sat glaring into the soft white glow of vanity lights moment-arily, shaking her head gently. Her face was flushed with the hot blood that had drained into it as she had laid down briefly, her eyes watery with stress and sadness.

'I think it could work.' Kirsten continued. 'At least while we wait to see what the box office can do. How could it hurt to at least to try? If it doesn't, we just don't post it and then consider it a meet and greet.'

'You want to get someone in here who is responsible for writing those vile things about me?'

'No. Someone who's written something nice. Clearly.'

'I don't know.'

'You could vet them.'

'I don't want any freaks in here.'

'Of course.'

'No crying or anything. People getting hysterical in front of me, I can't bear it. How are you even going to find someone?'

'I can look at the comments and posts from last night. We should also find someone with a bit of a decent following too so they can post about it.'

'Again, who?'

Kirsten was silent still and just glared up at Veronica. She sighed, looking directly into her eyes before going to her phone again. But before she could respond, Veronica leant in. 'Not that bloody drag queen in the picture on the thing?'

'Well…'

Veronica scoffed loudly before putting her face into her hands, rolling her head back and forth. 'She has a hell of a lot of followers,' Kirsten said gesturing with her phone.

'A lot of what?'

'Followers. People who follow her account.'

'What is a lot?'

'Fifty thousand.'

'Fifty thousand?' Veronica shouted, rotating herself around slowly. 'Fifty thousand people follow her on that thing.'

'Yes.'

'Fifty thousand people follow that enormous drag queen that was sat in the front row last night?'

'Yes.'

'How many people follow my account?'

'At the moment? About thirty thousand.'

'Is that good?'

'Considering you didn't have an account until two weeks ago, yes. It's good.'

'She dresses up like me and fifty thousand people watch that, but only thirty thousand follow me?'

'It doesn't really work like that but-'

'Fifty *thousand* people…' Veronica repeated under the breath.

For a moment it appeared as if Veronica were about to flip the table that she sat under. Fold each one of her long fingers under the bench and rip it from its position tucked against the soiled walls of the room and toss it across it, screeching. But she didn't move. She simply stood up, folded her arms and turned to glare at Kirsten. 'So what now? You're telling me you want to haul this drag queen in to talk to me? Here?'

Kirsten nodded. 'I think it could help yes.'

'You're really pushing this aren't you?'

'Pushing what?'

'This thing. With *them*,' pointing aggressively towards the door.

'Would you actually want to meet her?'

'What I want is more than twenty-five people sat in that theatre, darling. That's what I want...'

5:40pm

'Ready?' Kirsten asked, appearing slightly out of breath as she stood at the entrance to the dressing room. Veronica sighed and let her body fall forward towards the bench, then rose slowly and headed towards the mirrors, weaving her way through the haze of what would have been several, tensely drawn-in cigarettes beforehand. As she positioned herself once again at the centre of the floor mirrors, Kirsten noticed she had managed to not only get into the black sequinned gown herself but put on another, new layer of her makeup and change wigs, all in the short time that she had been gone. She watched Veronica gently dab at the black liner on the outside of her eyes with one finger and then at the red lip gloss on the edges of her mouth with another, tousle the ringlets of hair around her shoulders and tug and drape the fabric of the bottom half of the dress around her legs.

Even from the door and through the smoke that seemed to still lurk around her like the fog of a cold swamp, Kirsten was able to make out the show that was Veronica Lange slowly assuming the position of celebrity mannequin once again. She placed both hands on the tops of her hips, one of her shoulders twisted forward, the other fell back, the flesh of her cheeks were sucked in between the backs of her teeth, one leg was put out slightly through the slit of the gown and her chin tilted up towards the lights, eyes wide and lips puckered. When she finally looked back at through the mirror, she sighed heavily. 'Christ,' she said. 'Fine. Go.'

When Kirsten clicked the handle of the door down and puled it in, a deep, excited moan, came whirling through the room. Veronica winced into the mirrors as it bounced around the space, before eventually forming into some words. 'Hello?' it asked gently like a child creeping into an adult's room but with all the husk and gravel of an adult itself. With the silence and stillness that followed, Kirsten felt her jaw clench at the thought of having to intervene in the absence of Veronica's inability to even pretend to be happy to see their guest. But with one swift movement, she watched as she spun elegantly around to face the door, beaming with a smile showing almost every single tooth possible in her mouth, her eyes lit up like diamonds in candle light and her body twisted into position, angled, poised and ready. 'Shit,' the voice boomed again.

In the doorway, their enormous new guest stood deathly still, save for a large trembling hand that she had placed over her chest. Kirsten watched as Veronica's still wide, glistening eyes, scanned from the top of her stacked, brunette wigs to her immaculately painted face with its feathery lashes, dark eye shadow and perfectly drawn lips, down to the thick, lush folds of the black sequins gathered around her legs. She was holding a fistful of some of the dress tightly in her other hand, pulling some of the fabric above her ankles, exposing two enormous, clear plastic stilettos.

'Hello there sweet heart,' Veronica finally said, extending out a hand. 'Thank you for coming. It's a pleasure to meet you.'

'Hi,' she responded quickly and slightly too loud, before holding her hand to catch Veronica's, latching onto it gently. It enveloped the long, boney shape of her palm and fingers, before she raised it to her lips and kissed the air above it, a fraction away from making contact with the heavy paint on her lips.

'How sweet' Veronica twitched. 'Please, come. Have a seat.' She pulled her hand back quickly and turned to walk back into the room, before spinning back around again. 'Oh sorry, how rude of me. What's your name dear?'

'My name? Ah…' she mumbled, immediately reaching to anxiously toy with a piece of hair. She glanced over at Kirsten who folded her arms nervously and leant back against the wall.

'Oh come on now, don't be shy,' Veronica smiled, placing a hand on her shoulder and looking over at Kirsten. 'Tell us darling.'

'It's Sue.'

'Well, that's a lovely name. Susanne is it?

'Ah, not quite.'

'Well, what then?'

'It's Sue,' she said blushing hysterically. 'Sue Positry.'

'Oh,' Veronica scoffed, coughing slightly and yanking back her hand, like she had just landed her palm in something unpleasant. 'Right, well…'

'But Sue is fine, I don't mind.'

Veronica tried hard to keep smiling, straightening her back and shooting Kirsten a worried, stressed glance all at once. 'Sue it is then. Come, sit.' Sue mumbled back something inaudible and awkward that sounded like a Thank you as she settled into the deep grooves of the couch as gently as a person of that size could.

'I'm sorry if I seem a bit nervous.' Sue raised and shook both her hands before letting out an awkward laugh. 'Thank you so much for the opportunity to come and meet you here…' she trailed off, raising a hand to her face, waving it against her eyes as if to motion she was drying tears that were yet to fall. 'It's kind of a bit unbelievable to be honest…' She trailed off again, as the waving grew more manic.

'Oh how sweet. Kirsten dear, grab me those tissues would you?' Veronica gestured to the vanity before turning back to Sue. 'Now don't go crying like that, all that extraordinary makeup will start running.'

'Oh this?' Sue laughed, plucking several layers of the soft paper from the box that was held out in the space between them. 'Good luck. I haven't washed this off since last night. You know I went straight from your show here, to my gigs at The Cock and then at The Hole, fell in a heap at seven AM and then woke up to Ms Kirsten here asking me to come meet *you*. On Instagram, of all bloody places. I mean, it's been a bit of a day, you can imagine.'

'I'm sorry The Cock and the what?'

'The Hole.'

'The Hole?'

'Yeah it's a nightclub where I do my shows.'

'Well,' Veronica cleared her throat softly. 'Isn't that lovely.'

'Pretty late though. I don't usually go on till about one o'clock in the morning. I'm kinda new there still.'

'Well, we are *so* pleased you were able to muster up the energy to come then. Aren't we?' Veronica said, glaring at Kirsten with a harsh grin.

'I just love your dress Sue.' Kirsten smiled hard down on her, realising then and there that she had forgotten to suggest she might want to wear something different.

'Oh you're sweet, thank you.'

'Did you make it yourself?'

'This? I mean sort of, but no. It's not my design, but I made the alterations. Had to be taken out quite a lot as you can see. But between us girls,' she said straightening the fabric that was over her lap and arranging it around her ankles. 'I stole it.'

Kirsten went to scoff but covered her mouth once she saw the expression on Veronica's face drop. Still preoccupied with the ends of her gown and oblivious to the look of horror that was now bearing down upon her, Sue continued. 'You know,' she said, 'a few hundred dollars a gig and some free drink tickets doesn't go very far. You gotta make it work. And in all honesty, what's a big department store like David Jones gonna miss in one dress?' Kirsten nodded and smiled awkwardly. Veronica still hadn't moved and sat with her back arched in like the curve of a cobra, glaring down at the dress. 'Made sure it was a good one though,' Sue winked and nudged the air towards Kirsten. 'Carla Zampatti.'

'Kirsten,' Veronica said sharply, clearing her throat loudly towards her as she did. 'Can we begin?'

Kirsten leant in from the wall slowly and down towards them on the couch. 'Let's start with a shot of you both standing over there at the mirrors maybe?' Sue nodded and smiled broadly with Veronica doing her best to do the same as she gestured for her to lead the way to other side of the room. Kirsten watched as both of them hastily positioned themselves in their own unique, but clearly well choreographed ways of being photographed, whilst trying to accommodate the other in the shot; Sue making far more allowances for the presence of her idol than Veronica for her new guest.

Now she was before them and not hidden behind the dirty lens of a phone, Kirsten could see the significant amount of detail and precision Sue had given to altering her features and body to not just appear as a woman, but as specifically Veronica, and even more specifically Veronica as she was now. Her hair was stacked, thick and high just like Veronica's, with only a fleeting glimpse of it being a set of wigs from the faint line of mesh that sat pasted across her forehead, blushed and powdered over by the dense makeup. Her dress, again altered for her own shape, still had the cut and fit exactly as Veronica's body held hers. Despite the fact Sue's real eyes were almost impossible to see as they would sit in her face normally due to the extraordinary illusions she had constructed with the strokes of a brush, they still mimicked brilliantly Veronica's own; the subtle kink in the arch of the long thin eyebrows, the length and density of the lashes, then the accentuated cheekbones and sharpened chin that fell beneath them. It was all there.

But something only discernible through having both of them not just in the same room, but now side by side, was becoming increasingly more obvious to Kirsten as she watched on. Sue's figure was just slightly fuller than Veronicas, her chest (albeit rubber) was larger and rounder, her hips slightly wider and the dress she wore poured over her padded curves like thick honey dripping over round, polished fruit, as it wove its way down to her legs. She consumed the space in a way that was not only due to her height but with an intense sensuality that Veronica just did not and just could not. She had taken these small details of Veronica's hair, eyes, waist, hands and gestures and amplified them, but in a way that made her seem more Veronica and than Veronica was; a way that she could have only been decades earlier.

Kirsten edged closer and quickly took several shots on her phone before smiling up both of them. 'Great, thank you.'

'It's ok?' Sue asked excitedly before arriving quickly beside her. Veronica swanned passed them both dismissively and collapsed into the couch.

'It's great, I will post it in a second. Take a seat, so we can start,' Kirsten said covering her phone.

'So,' Veronica sighed, glaring at Kirsten who was now getting into position against the wall to begin filming. 'Our dear Ms *Pository.* Where should we begin?'

Sue shrugged and smiled, turning from Kirsten to Veronica giggling nervously. 'I'm not sure,' she said softly, before jumping up and slapping her palms on her lap. 'Oh, something I wanted to say first though was that I actually saw Amy a few months ago in New York, would you believe? At a nightclub in Brooklyn.'

'My Amy?' Veronica asked.

'Yeah, she was hosting a drag pageant.'

'A what?' Veronica sneered.

'Sorry not hosting, more like judging I guess. Like a competition thing.'

'Amy? Are you sure?'

'I think they must have got her in especially for it.'

'I see. And why was that then?'

Sue paused to look over and smile at Kirsten and then to Veronica again. 'Well because they were all dressed like you.'

'I'm sorry, what?' Veronica cleared he throat loudly. 'Who was?'

'The ah,' Sue paused briefly and held her hands together tightly. 'The drag queens were.'

'Dressed like me how?' Veronica said looking anxiously up to Kirsten.

'Like, I guess, characters from your films. Or just...' she trailed off and looked down at her gown. 'They have done it for a few years now. It's like an annual thing.'

Veronica's eyes widened and her lips pressed hard against her face. She clasped her hands together tightly and tried her best to smile, but instead fell into a harsh wince. 'Well, I had no idea.'

'You didn't? It's really fun. They call it LangeFest. Here, I can show you pictures if you like?' Sue turned to dive into her bag, oblivious to Veronica's squirms.

'No,' Veronica barked, leaning forward with her hand as if to try and shield herself from what was coming. Sue stopped mid-air, glaring back her with all the concern of a child caught with its hand inside a biscuit jar. Veronica fell back into the couch again and smiled with an anxious laugh. 'It's fine, I'm sure it was marvelous.'

Kirsten hunched over them from her position against the wall still. 'Did you enjoy the show last night Sue?' she asked quickly into the stressed awkwardness.

'Yes,' Veronica sighed heavily. 'What did you think of my show?'

Sue closed her eyes momentarily and appeared to try and steady herself before looking back up at them both and dramatically putting a hand over her large chest. 'I mean, you're asking the wrong person here, but I tell you, it's one of the greatest things I have ever seen on stage Ms Lange. If I am being truthful.'

'How sweet,' she beamed.

'You were radiant up there. I could have sat there all night listening to you. And the applause you got? Obviously you saw it too Ms Kirsten.' Kirsten nodded and smiled. 'I have to admit though,' Sue continued, leaning in towards Veronica. 'I did know most of the stories already, but that's just because I've read both your books, of course seen all your films, watched every interview you've ever done. But still, to hear you tell them live, was so special. An honor even I'd say. Truly, I never thought I'd ever be able to do that. And if I am perfectly honest, I don't think anyone ever thought they'd see you do something like this.' Sue turned to fuss with the ends of her gown, arranging them on the floor around her high-heels, leaving Veronica to stew on the comment briefly.

'Well,' Veronica laughed through her clenched teeth, before sighing heavily. 'Here I am!'

Kirsten cleared her throat loudly and glared down at Veronica, whose hands she saw now were clasped tightly together still with bright red, interwoven fingers and resting heavily in the canopy of the lap of her dress. Both women turned to watch Sue continue to play with various parts of her outfit, pinching and pulling at strands of beads and sequins, totally oblivious to the strange, tense silence that had descended upon the room. Veronica shot Kirsten a frustrated, wide eyed stare and lurched forward a fraction, silently begging for help.

'Sue why don't you begin by telling us a little bit about where you're from and what you do?' she said, steading her phone with both her hands.

'Oh sure. Well, I'm a country girl believe it or not,' she said smiling at Veronica. 'Grew up about ten hours drive west from here on a cattle station. I'd say the name of the town, but I promise you've never heard of it.'

'Cattle? Who'd have thought?' Veronica smiled hard.

'Yeah, it'd been in the family for about fifty odd years. It was a dairy farm at first. Pretty easy stuff. I used to love it. I love animals and cows are such gentle creatures. Quite beautiful really. Majestic I'd say even. But then y'know we fell on hard times with a few droughts back to back, some bad businesses decision and contracts. So it went from a dairy farm to an abattoir pretty quickly.'

'Oh god,' Veronica said, placing a hand on her chest.

'Yeah it's impressive how fast you can flip from one to the other. And it was tough at first, but I was happy to see my folks succeed finally. So then business was good again. We had good meat. Still do,' Sue said, nudging Veronica gently with her elbow, then cackling loudly. Veronica cleared her throat anxiously and shot stressed looks up towards Kirsten's phone again. Kirsten pulled it down slightly and tried to smile to calm her.

'And how did you get into this business then?' Veronica asked, scanning her outfit from top to bottom once again. 'Being a country boy and all?'

Sue smiled and tapped Veronica on her hand lightly. 'Country *lady*.' All Veronica could manage in response was a wince back at her. 'Well, I always had this urge to perform. But I guess I masked it with my bodybuilding.'

'Your what?'

'Bodybuilding. Used to compete professionally back about fifteen-twenty years ago. Wasn't bad at it you know?'

'How extraordinary.'

'And you know,' Sue said turning to Kirsten. 'I've realized that there is actually a lot in common between the two things.'

'Between being a drag queen and a bodybuilder?' Veronica asked quickly.

'I always thought so.'

'Right.'

'It's the fluorescent g-strings, the fake tan, all the posing and pageantry of it all,' Sue said trailing off. 'The body sculpting and all that. And it's exactly what drew me into it. The pageantry. But in reality I guess all I really wanted to do was put on a fucking dress,' she laughed nervously.

'And how did we progress to that?' Veronica asked, looking into Kirsten's phone anxiously.

'Took me till I was about thirty to realise it. I knew I was gay before though. I think I was sixteen or seventeen maybe. But all this?' she said, gesturing to her dress and down to her shoes. 'To go out in public like this? Took a bit longer. Because y'know being a bodybuilder in gay world, you are kinda top of the food chain. In a perverted sort of way. You get a lot of attention.'

'I imagine so.'

'You are like peak man, right? Big and muscled and all that. I hope it's changing now but back then, it's what everyone seemed to want to either be with or be like. But here I am now. Size thirteen, six-inch stripper heels, stacked human hair lace fronts, rubber titties. The full get up. And I couldn't be happier,' she said laughing softly again.

Veronica's expression oscillated from mildly curious to confused and repulsed, back and forth the whole time she was being spoke at. Sue took a pause and Veronica inhaled deeply, pursing her lips tighter as she scanned her outfit again, forgetting for a moment that she was being filmed and expected to offer some sort of response or reaction. Kirsten coughed again loudly to shake her from her silent assessment and she blinked quickly, shook her head and clapped her hands together loudly.

'Ok, great. So, shall we talk about the show some more?'

'Yes, the show!' Sue beamed.

'Could you tell us something in particular you liked about last night?' Kirsten asked, leaning in with her phone closer to Sue's face. 'Maybe the bits you enjoyed the most?'

'Oh god you put me on the spot now. Let me think,' she said tilting her head and stroking her chin gently. 'Ok, so firstly I think the opening, I absolutely *loved* the opening. That video montage you had on the backdrop screen thing, before you came on stage. All those amazing old video clips. That was incredible. And that song you had playing also? Say Goodbye to Hollywood, by Bette Midler?'

'Oh yes,' Veronica smiled, beginning to shuffle in the couch.

'I actually do it some times in my own shows, would you believe? She's such an icon. So camp too. I do this whole skit dressed as Glen Close in *Sunset Boulevard*, with the dressing gown and the turban and those eyebrows, running around the floor of the club screaming the lyrics to the song. It's hilarious. Honestly, please come some time. The boys would fall over themselves to see you there. Especially at The Hole.'

'I bet,' Veronica mumbled.

'Say goodbye to Hollywood,' Sue began to sing softly, cutting Veronica off. She closed her eyes briefly before turning to face Kirsten. 'Say goodbye to Hollywood. Say, goodbye my baby…' She continued on, gently clicking her fingers to a beat that existed inside her head only. She turned to Veronica who was smiling, but appeared to be edging further back into the armrest. Eventually she closed her eyes and began to sway gently on the couch, her long hair waving back and forth down her shoulders in motion with her huge body. Veronica took a deep breath and glanced up at Kirsten who shot her an equally manic look straight back. She exhaled loudly again and smiled. 'It's not a Bette Midler song,' she said, slicing through Sue's slow descent into a musical day dream. Sue stopped swaying immediately and glared curiously at Veronica.

'It's not what?'

'Say Goodbye to Hollywood is a Billy Joel song.'

'Billy Joel?'

'Yes. Billy Joel.'

'Are you sure?'

'Yes.'

'But it's so camp? It can't be.'

'It is.'

'Surely it's Bette Midler?'

'She did that to it.'

'Did what?'

'Better Midler did that to it. Made it camp. The original is not camp.'

Sue stroked the underneath of her jawline gently nodding as she did. 'She does cover a lot of other people's songs I guess. But you used the Bette Midler version last night didn't you?'

Veronica looked deadpan into Sue's face and sighed. 'No.'

All three of them sat in silence while Kirsten fussed with her
phone, clearly having stopped recording for the moment. 'I tell
you what?' Sue said finally, jumping slightly towards Veronica.
'That photo of you and Liza Minelli and Jerry Hall at the
Oscar's was just the tits. I loved it so much.' Veronica smiled.
'That was one I never actually saw before.'

'Oh good, I'm glad.'

'Did anything else happen that night?'

'With what?'

'With you, and Liza and Jerry.'

'What do you mean?' Veronica trailed off, suddenly looking
uncomfortable and tense.

'Or any other stories about Liza? I just love her.'

Kirsten watched as Veronica's back arched further inward and
she pursed her lips together tightly. She cleared her throat twice
and made several attempts to try and avoid eye contact with
either of them by touching and playing with her hair and tugging
at her dress and the couch. Just as she was about to look up, Sue
threw her head back and cackled. 'Christ, sorry who am I?' she
said, shaking herself and putting her hands to her face. 'Two
minutes in and I'm already making demands. Maybe I should
leave you both to it. I'm sure you have a million things to do
before you go on again tonight. Let me know if you wanna take
anymore pics. But let me just grab my bag first.'

She began twisting her torso about and patting around the cushions for any sign of her things. Veronica watched her in silence,
appearing first totally at ease with allowing her to leave quietly.
She scanned her enormous, sequinned body up and down as she

moved about, grabbing and arranging herself but just before she stood, Kirsten let out another loud cough, snapping Veronica out of her gaze immediately and dousing her with a wide eyed, stressed urgency that she personally ensure their guest remained right where she was.

'Please' she said finally, lurching towards Sue and placing a hand over her lap. 'Stay. We have plenty of time.'

'Are you sure?' Sue said half-heartedly.

'Of course. It's fine. Stay.' Sue eased her way back into the couch once again and sat beaming at Veronica.

'Ok,' she smiled, suddenly looking ashamed she had even offered to go. 'So how long have you actually known Liza?' she asked excitedly and before she had even sat down fully again.

Veronica sighed heavily but only through the gaps in her lips. She looked out the corner of her eyes as Kirsten folded her arms with the phone now up again. 'We met in a recording studio in New York. I think in seventy-eight or seventy-nine,' she said, scratching her neck. 'I was dating one of the guys who I think might have worked there at the time and I just happened to be around when she was in one day, we got chatting and I guess that was it.'

'Wow,' Sue beamed up at Kirsten. 'And when was the last time you saw her?'

'Oh, I don't think I could tell you darling. She's a busy woman. We are both busy, you know, life goes on.'

'Do you two still speak now?'

Veronica exhaled loudly. 'No, we don't.'

Sue nodded politely and appeared to try and smile while sinking back into the couch slightly. She turned to glare into Kirsten's phone with the same strained expression of thanks before bowing down to fuss with her dress nervously as another dull silence descended between them all. Kirstren looked over her screen at her and sighed quietly.

'Veronica why don't you tell Sue that story you told me about Liza the other day?' she said quickly.

'Which one dear?' Veronica replied through her teeth.

'The one about her performing at the Wizard of Oz charity benefit thing. That's a good one.'

Veronica looked over to Sue who she saw was now slightly open mouthed and with her hands clasped together in a tight prayer over her lips. She smiled back and took a deep breath.

'Oh, I ah, I don't know darling. I don't want to bore Ms Positry here.'

Sue snapped her neck back and cackled loudly. 'Ah, when Ms Positry is bored, Ms Positry will let you know, don't worry.'

'It's really not that exciting darling I promise you. I can't even remember half of it. I don't know what she is referring to really even. Let's just carry on with the show shall we?'

'It was the one about her on stage with the cocai-'

'Ok, ok,' Veronica snapped, cutting her off and waving her hand across her face. 'Yes, I know. Ok.'

Sue clapped excitedly, shooting manic smiles into Kirsten's phone and then back to Veronica again. 'But, this one is not for the cameras OK?' She winked at Sue who giggled gently. Kirsten edged back and put her phone away. 'Just between us girls.' Sue made the motion of zipping her lips shut and then pulled her knees in together and leaned on her hands.

Veronica tapped her cheek and looked to the ceiling. 'There was this night back in the late eighties, maybe eighty-eight, where Liza was booked as a headliner for this charity event that was also a thing to mark some anniversary of the film for the Wizard of Oz. I remember there being lot of buzz around her being there, fans of her mother's were going a bit crazy about it. And so she shows up, but tonight, for some godforsaken reason, she decides to make it the first day of work for her new PA. This tiny little thing that was plucked from who knows where by her agency to help her get about. I have no idea how old she actually was either, but I remember at the time she looked like she was fresh from a girl scout jamboree. Poor thing, standing there with a clipboard, all doe-eyed and shaking as all these incredibly famous people milled about Liza and her entourage. So the night is going well, I am backstage with Jerry Hall, waiting for it all to begin and people start showing up for the show. Liza is there and for all intents and purposes this PA girl is doing a fine job, save for one thing.'

'Oh no,' Sue leaned in. 'What?'

'No one told her she was responsible also for Liza's, ah, how should we put it...' Veronica paused and looked over her shoulder, before raising her fingers into air quotations. '*Supply.*'

'Supply?'

'Yes.'

Sue squinted at her briefly, curiously tilting her head before tapping one of her nostrils with the end of a long acrylic nail. 'Yes, that,' Veronica nodded.

'Right.'

'Well this girl scout is beside herself when she is all but thrown out of the dressing room and told to find something there and then, otherwise the night's most anticipated performer would categorically not be going on.'

'Oh shit.'

Veronica looked up at Kirsten who was smiling now as she leant further into the wall, glaring back at Sue. 'Luckily one of the lighting guys who saw her crying on the floor outside the room had some paltry amount on him which was promptly handed to her boss and really that should have been the end of it. But, in true form, Liza insisted that more be found at once or again, she would refuse to go on. So the lighting guy and the PA are now scrambling around with about forty-five minutes left until curtain trying to find a more sizeable quantity for Liza in order for her to sing. It's just chaos. But word gets around about what is going on with other people in the show and after a while, so it happens, a man fairly well known in that department, has arrived in the theatre. Someone clocks him and sends the PA over to him immediately and she begins pleading, and I mean like properly begging for him to help. But he isn't there for this sort of business. He has tickets the show would you believe? Still they carry on pleading and begging with him to hand something over at any cost. He considers it for a minute and obviously sensing their desperation, says to the PA he will hand it over, but only on one condition…'

'Oh god, what?'

'If Liza sings Somewhere Over the Rainbow as the last song of the night.'

'Ok, that's odd.'

'But anyone who knows, knows that she categorically does *not* sing that song. She never has in public, except maybe once as a kid, but it's just known that she won't sing it. She is asked almost every single night she goes on stage, even now, to sing it and it's the same reaction. She says the same thing, Oh honey that song's not my song to sing, it's my Mother's, she says, and she sticks to it. Fifty odd years in the business and she's never done it. No matter who asks. And this guy, he knew it. But still he dug his heels in. Some mad Judy Garland fan clearly, and when the message got back to Liza she promptly told him to where to go.'

'So what happened? She didn't go on?'

'No, somehow they managed to convince her to get up and do her numbers and she was electrifying as always, but just as she's getting to the last few bars of her final song, she clocks the guy in the audience. He is this tall, very pale thing, skinny as a rake with a thick blonde moustache. She must have recognised him from something before. Maybe she used him once for something. And he's holding a bunch of roses, obviously ready to throw them onto the stage after she's done.'

'What an asshole.'

'So she's seen the guy, he's seen her see him and as she's wrapping up the show, he very subtly pulls out a small bag of stuff and dangles it in front of him in perfect sight for her to see. She sees it and stops dead. Her eyes are wide and you can see she is totally fixated on it for a second. Suddenly she turns to the band and whispers something to them. They are briefly stunned but then arrange themselves again quickly and she returns to the front of the stage and just starts. She does the most heart wrenching version of Somewhere Over the Rainbow you've ever heard. Everyone was a total wreck at the end of it. Crying, on their feet clapping madly. Once she was done, flowers start piling up from the audience on the stage; falling from the dress circle and up from the floor. The crowd was ecstatic, but the whole time she held her focus on the blonde guy in the second row. Not moving, barely even smiling. And sure enough, true to his word, he shoves the little bag of powder into the bouquet and hurls it on stage where it lands directly at her feet. She bends down to sweep it up, waves at the audience and bolts off stage.'

'Ha!' Sue, cackled and fell back into the couch, with both hands over her mouth. 'Wow.'

'So, there you go,' Veronica said looking smug, smiling. 'That's the Liza story.'

'Ms Lange you gotta tell that story in your show! It's wild. The guys would love it.'

Veronica smiled politely and cocked her head to the side. 'Oh no dear, that's just ah,' she trailed off slightly before shaking her head. 'No. There's enough in there already I think.'

'Truly.'

Veronica smiled again and touched Sue patronisingly on the leg before laughing quietly. 'No, no,' she said, trailing off again, waving her hand dismissively in Sue's face.

Finally relenting, Sue leant back, rubbing her stomach gently, before mumbling. 'I am so sorry, do you mind if run to the bathroom quickly?' she asked anxiously. 'I didn't want to interrupt your story, but I really should go.'

'Oh, ah, yes. Please. Go,' Veronica said gesturing quickly towards the door as if she was about to go right there on the floor.

'I won't be long. I'm sorry.' Sue rose, letting her dress fall gently to the floor and started for the corridor.

'It's just down a bit and to the right,' Kirsten said as she passed her. 'Take your time.'

'Thank you. God this is embarrassing. Sorry.' She stumbled out, gently scraping the ceiling with the top of her wig.

When the door clicked shut softly, Kirsten let out a long, exhausted sigh and turned to smile at Veronica but stopped half way when she saw what was facing back at her.

'Christ's sake,' Veronica screamed, bolting up from the couch and over to her cigarette box. As she lit one, she hurled the metallic lighter across the table and watched it collide with several other things on the other side of the bench. 'What was that?'

'What was what?'

'You and pushing that bloody Liza Minelli shit, Kirsten. Honestly.'

'I was just trying to make sure she was interested still. I thought we were losing her.'

'We couldn't even record it! That's the whole reason we are doing this. What is the point of it all if we don't get anything to put up? To get these people in those damn seats?'

'Yeah why didn't you want me to record you telling it?'

'Because it's not true!'

'Isn't it?'

'No! It's just some stupid story people made up about her.'

'I didn't know that.'

'No, I imagine you didn't,' Veronica said as she blasted out an aggressive plume of smoke towards her.

Kirsten slumped gently against the wall and folded her arms as Veronica turned to face the mirrors on the floor again. The more she watched on through the haze, the more she began to notice the change Veronica's expression was currently going through as she stared deeper into herself. Something she had noticed even in the the early days of their meetings was this extraordinary talent she had for pulling, moving and contorting parts of the skin in her face that made her seem instantly more poised, put together and rested. She would press her eyebrows down and push them up towards her temples, scrunch the flesh over her cheekbones up also and then pull it back towards her ears. She would curl her top lip up and her bottom lip down and then pull the skin across her mouth and breathe gently through it as she spoke. It was, like most of her physical nuances, painstakingly subtle to anyone who didn't know her well. But even after their short time together, Kirsten was beginning to notice the vast differences between her looks when she was on, versus when she was off. When she was Veronica Lange, the actress, Academy Award winner, celebrity and star versus the human, flawed, tired, frustrated and weary.

'Does it really matter though if it's not true?' Kirsten said quietly. Veronica glared at her curiously for a moment through the disappearing cloud between them. 'What?' she spat back, irritated instantly.

'Well, she was hanging on to it, wasn't she? She believed it. What does it matter if it's not true?'

Veronica sighed loudly, as she shook her head and turned around to face the mirrors again. 'How much longer is this going to take?'

'As long as we want I guess?' Kirsten said softly. Veronica watched Kirsten again for a moment longer in silence, eyeing her up and down, squinting, appearing to try see through her more than at her, to see what she was meaning rather than saying. She sucked in deep on the remainder of the cigarette and held it all tightly in her chest, before blowing it all out through her nose.'Is that what this has all been reduced to, is it? Making up stories about fucking Liza Minelli to sell tickets to forty something year old drag queens?'

Kirsten shrugged, shuffling on her feet. 'I think they just want you to be a star Veronica, I don't think they really care if what you tell them is true or not. I don't think it matters.'

'Is that so? Well-'

A heavy but still polite knock came through the other side of the door, cutting her off. Kirsten watched as Veronica 's eye's rolled twice in two full rotations before she strutted over to the corner of the room. She glanced at a silver wrist watch strapped tightly around the end of her thin arm. 'We have less than two hours to fill that theatre again. I suggest you come up with a better idea than recording me telling queer bedtimes stories to drag queens to do it.'

As Kirsten moved to open the door, without even a pause to steady herself or a brief moment of contemplation before she was back on again, Veronica was poised and firmly back in position of being ready to be admired. 'Well, that was quick darling!' she beamed, as she spun around, holding a hand out and gesturing for Sue to join her back on the couch. Sue had stopped at the door, smiling and blushing heavily.

'Oh yeah, well when you're in a gown like this, you don't really need to, y'know...' She motioned towards her crotch, making a scooping gesture with her hand between her legs. Kirsten laughed, covering her mouth quickly with her phone. Veronica watched on struggling to hold back how mortified she was becoming, but managed to smile regardless.

'So thrilled to have you back, aren't we? Come, sit,' Veronica said, patting the space on the couch beside her where she had just settled. 'We'd just love to get to know a little bit more about you and your background and,' Veronica looked up at Kirsten. 'All those sorts of things.' Sue followed as she was told and fell into the couch once again.

'Kirsten?' Veronica beamed up to her. 'Any more questions you might have in particular for our gorgeous guest?'

Kirsten fussed about with her hands in her pockets for a moment, before pulling out her phone and positioning herself against the wall again. 'Well, I was going to ask you Sue, if you might have a question you want to ask Veronica?' She smiled down at her, feeling Veronica's burning glare on her the entire time. Sue smiled broadly back at her and then looked down at her knees. They bounced up and down nervously as she appeared briefly deep in thought. Her eyes were closed tightly as she rose her head to face Veronica once again and leaned in closer. 'I don't have a question, it's more of a statement if that's OK?' she asked looking back and forth to both of them. Kirsten nodded gently as she pushed the phone closer towards them. 'Ms Lange, I wanted to tell you that for the record, I actually loved that film…' Sue said as she placed a hand over one of Veronica's. 'Which film darling?'

'*Isabella.*'

'Oh, I see.'

'I actually loved it a lot. Despite what everyone says.'

'Well, Sue Positry, I get the impression darling there isn't much I could do that you wouldn't love.' Veronica laughed gently as Sue smiled, pulling back her hand, blushing slightly.

'Despite everything that happened, do you think it's a good film?'

'No, I don't.'

'Ok. But that's just because of what other people did to it, right?'

'Yes.'

'The producers and those investors. Your ex-husband was responsible I think for a lot of the terrible marketing also, wasn't he?'

'He was, yes.'

'I read about it in your book. About how they kept changing the directors and the locations, so the budget blew out.' Veronica nodded. 'And then when they realised most of the footage was unusable once it was done…'

'Yes.'

'… so they just kind of shoved it out quickly to try and recoup some of the costs and when they thought they knew it was a going to flop, they promoted it as some campy B-film comedy thing which it was never meant to be. Those posters of you in that scene, screaming with your tiara falling off, it wasn't meant to be like that, was it?'

'No, it wasn't.'

'The book it was based on though, it was a masterpiece, wasn't it?'

'Yes.'

'What did the author say about it? The film I mean. Did you ever hear from her about it all?'

'She blamed me, like the rest of them.'

'How could they turn a story about the last queen of Spain, into something so strange and kitsch?'

'I don't know, but they more than succeeded.'

'All that aside Ms Lange, I thought you were dazzling. Through all that effort to trash the story and the film and you, you shone through, still.'

'Im glad you think so darling, thank you. But you'd be the only one.'

'Well me and the hundreds of other people on their feet last night also, right?'

Veronica smiled. 'You came with some friends did you?'

'Well no, I actually came alone. But I ended up knowing half the theatre just from my work. And the other half ended up knowing me. So it was like a bit of a family affair.' Veronica nodded along politely. 'It's a bit like that at these things around here sometimes.' Sue paused for a moment, taking in a deep breath. 'You don't talk about the film in your show I noticed…' Veronica shook her head gently, as Sue watched she nodded along sympathetically. 'The producers and the studio heads and the director and everyone running the film, they were all men weren't they?' Veronica nodded again slowly. She looked up at Sue and for the first time since they met, appeared to allow her face to soften, to relax and breath as it would normally. She inhaled through her nose but just as she went to speak, Kirsten leant forward.

'So, Sue,' she said loudly holding her phone up, her voice cutting through the sweet and sincere calm that has been building between them. 'What about when you first came across some of Veronica's work? Maybe the first time you saw her on screen? How old were you?'

Veronica and Sue both turned to face her at the same time, with the same look of minor astonishment. Sue smiled quickly enough, turning back to Veronica. 'Well that's an easy one,' she said, placing a hand back on her lap. 'Clear as day I can remember it. I must have been about eight or nine years old at the time. And you know when they used to have a film on Channel Seven every Friday night, after the footy? Like the old ones though, never anything new,' she said looking at Kirsten while Veronica squirmed. 'I'd sit there on the floor, not really paying much attention to what was going on, I was always just happy to be allowed to stay up so late. Usually it was some stupid John Candy film or National Lampoons something. And when it came on I always thought, What is this? Why are they watching this crap? But I was a good kid. I kept quiet. I was well behaved. So this one night I'm there watching, again not really paying attention, and it turns out it's *Goodbye Istanbul*. Like, of all your films to start with Ms Lange.'

'It's a good one darling, yes.'

'So that first scene where you come into the ambassador's office during that meeting with all the heads of state, dressed in that white power suit and the pink scarf? I'd never seen anything like that. Women didn't wear suits where I grew up, you see. I never even seen a shoulder pad on someone before. My mother bless her, is an angel, but she thinks washing her hair is the equivalent of a spa day. So immediately I'm just totally and utterly captivated by you.'

'Thank you,' Veronica sighed.

'And then it just went on from there. That shot of you being taught how to belly dance in the desert? It's literally burned into the back of my eye lids. The black silhouette of your body and those hips curling and turning against that dark orange sunset. I just...' Sue trailed off, fanning herself with her hands. Veronica smiled and started to slouch slightly, falling softly into the couch. 'And that was it I think. I'm the kind of person that when I see something that sparks my curiosity I just dive in head first. I'm like at the video store in town, arms full of plastic VHS cassettes of all your films, I'm at the local library pulling your worn biographies off the shelves, ripping pages out of my mother's glossy magazines, quietly slicing out articles from the newspaper. Anything that even mentioned you in passing, I was just devouring. But,' Sue mumbled and paused to nervously finger some of her jewellery. 'All obviously in secret. It's not like I could tell anyone about it or put your posters up or anything,' she laughed to herself softly.

'How come?' Kirsten asked, immediately hiding behind her phone again as she did.

Sue scoffed. 'Well, what do you think? A cattle station isn't exactly a sympathetic place for exploring ones creative outlets, is it? These little gay boys, sitting out in the middle of nowhere with nothing but a TV and a few dusty video's to keep them dreaming.' Kirsten nodded and smiled gently. 'You are part of that dream Ms Lange.'

'What do you mean darling?' Veronica asked as she sat up.

'I think at that age when you're gay and you know you're gay, you don't just watch movies, you sort of force yourself into them as a way of escaping the world a bit.' Veronica watched on silently as Sue began to curl into herself slightly, not making eye contact anymore, just nervously flicking her fingers and toying with her gown. 'And I guess like a kid who think's or knows he's straight, he can watch a movie, any movie and just get up after it's finished and say, That was nice and then go back to his life easily, because it's their world isn't it? The one we all live in. But when a little queer kid watches a movie, especially when they know who they are already and that the world is not for them, they go *into* that movie, into that book or whatever it is, as a respite from that world and they're lost inside it. And you're right there with them. So when they see you in real life, it's hard to forget that. It's hard to not see you as the character that we latched onto as some thing that lead us away from the shittiness of our circumstances. Even if you are just walking in the street or at some restaurant. I watch your films now and I cry...'

'Oh darling, don't, please.'

'No I cry because I think I see myself sat there watching them, so young, and I know what that boy was going through and the stress and anxiety of it all. But I cry because I am through it and on the other side and I know it's going to be ok. And I cry because I want to reach through that screen and shake him and say, It's going to be ok. That's why I cry when I watch it. And that's why I cry when I see you. I imagine that's why any of us would cry when they see you really...' Veronica nodded silently, patting Sue lightly on the hand. 'I wasn't ever really able to properly express myself as a kid, so my expression was just silently putting myself right beside you in the movies you made.'

'Do your parents know about you?' Veronica asked.

'About me being gay? I mean yeah by now I guess so. But this?' Sue said looking down at her dress. 'I dunno...'

'Ok.'

'There was this one time though, when I was pretty young, this incident, that I think might have made them realise, or least consider it. But now, I don't know.'

'Do you want to tell us what happened?' Kirsten asked, edging in closer. Sue glared up at her nervously and then down at her clenched hands sitting in her lap.

'I mean, I can, but are you sure wanna film it?' Sue laughed into the phone.

'If that's ok with you?'

'Yeah, I mean go ahead. I got nothing to hide,' she said smiling gently before turning back to Veronica. 'So, like I said, that scene in the desert, of you dancing in *Goodbye Istanbul,* it never left me. I just thought, that it was the absolute epitome of what it meant to be a woman. Of like femininity, glamour and seduction and all that. And I knew I was gay because I didn't want to be with her. You, I mean. That woman up there on the screen, I wanted to be *like* her. And that was the end of it. Because it was like she existed on another planet. I would walk around my parent's property, it was big and I guess there was beauty in there somewhere, in the landscape. But it was machinery. Men in jeans and torn shirts. Cars and petrol. Cow shit. Dogs and mud. There was nothing. No sign of the kind of beauty I was seeing in the film anywhere. So I sort of just retreated into myself. I created this world where I could turn the things around me into what I needed.'

'That's very sweet dear,' Veronica said, starting to look slightly bored.

'So by this stage I was working in the packing rooms of the meat shop. After we went from a dairy farm to an abattoir, I would get pocket money wrapping the meat and I know it sounds gross, but I loved it because I was alone. No one would bother me and I would sing and dance about, say out loud lines from films in my head. Your films, Ms Lange. I would dance like you danced in

Goodbye Istanbul. I'd snap my hips back and forth to that quick, tinny beat of those drums but dressed in my rubber boots, those awful white lab coats and a hair net, all stained with blood and guts, just darting across the room holding sawn off bits of cow carcasses. But one day, when I was working on the sausage section, I got really into it. Like *really* into it. And I dunno what came over me,' Sue hunched into herself slightly, suddenly looking shy. Veronica shot Kirsten a concerned look but remained silent. Kirsten continued on filming.

'I was reciting lines from *Goodbye Istanbul* and I just picked up a few strings of beef sausages and draped them around my shoulders like the golden shawl you had on, and started prancing around. There were mirrors all through the room that I would just swan up to and mouth the words that you said to the man in the desert as you're dancing for him. Those big beautiful lips of yours puckered and your eyes dark and smoked with all that eyeliner and shadow. And I guess I just got a bit carried away. I grabbed two massive sirloin steaks and some Cling Wrap and gave myself a huge set of tits. I just lost myself in the moment.'

'Ok,' Veronica said quietly through her teeth, as she watched Sue slowly cower further into the couch, shooting Kirsten awkward glances directly into the lens of her phone.

'I didn't realise the door was open at the back of the room. My father had walked in with a new stack of T-bones freshly sliced and ready for me to wrap. And there's his son, sausages draped around his arms and a size triple D breast plate made from some of his finest cuts, twirling about, singing.'

Veronica gritted her teeth more and wrung her hands together tightly, with more and more manic glances being shot into the phone hovering above her. 'I just froze when I saw him in the mirror. Froze. I couldn't move,' Sue sobbed softly. 'All I could do was hold my pose. My arms up in the air, my hips cocked to one side. The sausages draped around my shoulders and down my forearms. And slowly I saw him approach from behind. I thought he would just smack me on the back of the head and tell me to quit fucking around at work. But he didn't say anything. He just stood there, holding those bloody T-bones, looking like he had just seen me murder someone.'

Slowly and gently, Sue started to cry softly into her hands, but stopped just shy of pressing them against her face. Just as Veronica motioned to reach for the tissues again, Sue snapped her neck back up to face her, this time with huge black streaks of makeup pouring down her cheeks. 'And then,' she wailed, 'after a few moments, he moved towards me, but instead of smacking me, he places a hand on my lower back and pushes me very gently into the next room where we had another set up to deal with the waste. And very calmly, still without saying a single word, he bends down to switch on this massive incinerator, that's basically just a big fire pit. We both stand there, watching the flames grow bigger and bigger and finally he pulls his arm out and just points into the pit. I'm crying my eyes out by this stage right. A total mess. But I still manage to untangle my arms from the sausages, slowly unwrap the steaks from my chest and then toss everything into the flames. I was bawling, properly hysterical at the sight of my beautiful fantasy all cooking away underneath my nose. To this day, I still can't stand the smell of red meat burning on a grill. Truly, it brings me to tears. More tears...' Sue sniffed, fanning her hands over her enormous eye lashes, waving the tissue along with them also. 'God and now look at me. A mess. Again!' She pressed her fingers against the under sections of her eyes trying her best to not rub her makeup more than it had already been ruined, and to laugh all at once. 'Sorry,' she blubbered. 'I can't believe I just told you that story. I don't think I've told anyone that before.'

'Don't apologise, it's very kind of you to share it. Thank you,' Kirsten said, reaching for some more tissues from another box on Veronica's vanity and quietly putting her phone away.

'I dunno, I think it's just a bit of a combination of not much sleep, bit of a champagne hangover, and meeting you Ms Lange. You have no idea what you meant to me as a little queer kid for all those years.' Sue let her sobbing swallow up her words again before clearing her throat and shaking her head to steady herself.

Veronica didn't do anything but smile. She didn't move, she didn't lean forward to offer a hand to help, or any words to comfort and calm her at any moment. All she seemed to be able to manage was to smile at her. Not in a way that meant anything other than she was simply acknowledging that she was present and listening. 'Won't be much use for that will it?' Sue said, gesturing to Kirsten's phone hanging from her pocket, blowing her nose.

'For what?'

'For your social media or anything?'

'Oh,' Kirsten said before smiling awkwardly. 'It's fine.'

'Would you mind if...' Sue mumbled, blowing her nose loudly again. 'Would you mind if I laid down just a minute?'

'What do you mean?' Kirsten asked.

'I just always get a bit light headed when I get upset like this. The wigs and the pads and the shoes probably aren't helping either. Just to settle myself down a bit? Sorry. You don't wanna see someone my size collapse in a small space like this. It's not pretty.'

Veronica jumped up immediately as if something had just bitten her from behind and stood nervously at the door next to Kirsten.'Yes of course. Go ahead,' Kirsten said, gesturing to the now empty couch. 'Help yourself.'

'Thank you both. Sorry about this.'

Kirsten and Veronica stood in silence, side by side, watching Sue in her heavy jewellery and piles of wigs laying her enormous, bedazzled body flat on the small couch. Her large feet, still shoved tightly into the plastic stripper heels she had walked in with, stacked clumsily on the arm rest and her hands with their long nails folded over one another across her stomach. She looked up to shoot them both a quick, thankful smile before closing her eyes, taking a few long deep breaths and then letting herself fade into a light sleep.

Veronica turned to Kirsten and raised both her arms up and then let them flap down against her side, but stopped short of allowing the inevitable slap that would have followed. 'What in the fucking Christ was that?' she growled, trying her best to whisper and shout at the same time. Kirsten didn't respond. She was still entirely fixated the sight of Sue's body drifting slowly off to sleep beneath her.

'You wanted a story, Kisten? Well you bloody got one! Didn't think she was going to go into some deep, psychological trauma about her dressing up in meat and then having her father bbq the outfit in front of her, did you?'

Kirsten shook her head and winced to try and snap herself back to the present. Veronica leant right into her face and smiled with just her teeth. 'So what do we do now, huh?'

'Well we got the photo from before,' Kirsten said, her voice breaking slightly. 'She can post it and we just see how that goes and maybe when she wakes up-'

'When she *wakes up*. When she bloody *wakes up*. My god.' Veronica stormed off to the other side of the room, arms folded and glaring down at Sue who had now started to snore gently. 'How long are we expected to wait for her to wake up? And what if this doesn't work? Is that it?'

Kirsten was silent again. All she seemed to be able to do was glare from Veronica's eyes back over her shoulder to Sue's enormous body laying in state. With each passing second she felt Veronica's hot urgency for a a quick answer pouring into her and her inability to give one, fueling an urge to lunge straight for her neck with both hands curled around it. But once Kirsten looked back to her one final time and sighed with a all the exhaustion and defeat of a battle weary horse, all she ended up managing to do was close her eyes and exhale heavily. 'Please, check the tickets again,' she said.

'What?' Kirsten shot back quickly, still not quite sure if she should bolt from the room.

'Check the tickets again.'

'Ok, but-'

'Check the tickets again.' Veronica pushed each word through her all but entirely sealed lips as if each one were worthy enough of its own sentence. Trembling slightly, Kirsten turned to her phone and quietly began swiping away at the screen. After a few seconds she looked up nervously. 'Twenty-eight,' she said softly.

'Twenty-eight?'

'Yes.'

'Twenty-eight tickets have sold?' Veronica slumped down into her chair, letting her face fall fully into her hands. She sat in silence breathing into her palms heavily. 'Well, that's it then, I guess, isn't it?'

'What's it?'

'The show's over. Pull it.'

'What do you mean *pull it*? What does -'

'I won't go on like this, Kirsten. I won't.'

'Oh Veronica come on…'

'Come on, what?' she mumbled into her hands before looking up again. Kirsten was silent. 'Would you do it?' Veronica leaned in, her arms folded tightly now across her body. 'Would you go on stage to perform for not even thirty people? Like this? In there?' When Kirsten didn't respond, Veronica pouted her lips further, raising her eyebrows and her nose towards her. 'I didn't think so.'

'We can still try and get some of this stuff up online. Like the photo.'

Veronica laughed loudly, shaking her head aggressively. 'A photo,' she mumbled. 'A bloody photo is what is going to fix this. Of me. And *her*…'

'It might work.'

'It won't, I promise you. I won't do it darling. It's done, ok? I'm sorry. How could I? These people and their camera phones. Snapping away at the sea of empty seats as I am up there pouring out my heart and soul, alone. I won't do it Kirsten. I'm sorry but it's over. *They* won.'

'Who won?'

'Them!' Veronica growled, flinging her arm out towards Sue behind her on the couch.

'Veronica, you can't go packing it in now after one night.'

'I know,' she said waving her hand in the air dramatically. 'How sad really, to think I could be taken seriously by the world at this age. To think that they would still want to listen to anything I have to say.'

'Let's just cancel tonight and then spend all day tomorrow going-'

'Cancel everything.'

Kirsten dropped her face into her hands and shook it gently for a moment, taking a deep breath in. 'Veronica we can't do that.'

'You're going to have to darling if I'm not here aren't you? What are you going to do if I'm not here to perform for them?'

'I think you'd be making a huge mistake.'

'Would I?'

'Yes.'

'Well I don't, darling. I tap out of this, you still get your cheque. The money still comes. People will be paid. But if I go ahead, I stand there performing at no one, what's that cost to me? People on fucking Twitter and their TimeOut reviews.'

'Just cancel tonight then. We'll say you're sick or something. We can tell them you've lost your voice and then spend all day tomorrow getting the word out, discount the tickets and send out complimentary ones even. Try again on your social media.'

'But the reviews darling. The reviews. It's useless. It won't help.'

'Fuck the reviews.'

'Yes, fuck the reviews,' Veronica sighed, arching her shoulders over the back rest of the chair. 'I'd say fuck the critics too, but there are no more critics are there? These people are the critics now. These tiny little apps on your tiny little phones and your Wikipedia, and your TripAdvisors and fucking *armchair* theatre reviewers. Liking, hating, liking, hating. Like some gladiatorial combat they decide fates, destroy whole careers, whole lives. Thumbs up or thumbs down. Well darling,' she sighed. 'Let them have it.'

'There's is still time.'

'What is it now? Six forty-five? I'm due on stage in an hour. What is there left to try? Go out in the street and start ripping people from the sidewalk and shoving them into a seat? Who's going to do that? You? It can't be that hard to find a few of these men you're so obsessed with lurking around outside, can it? It's the theatre district after all. The gay bars shouldn't be too far off darling. I'll lasso fifty of them with a promise of a washed up, double Academy Award winner in, what did the review say? Bob Mackie-esque couture? Camp caricatures and camp stories, camp, camp, bloody camp!'

'The reviews weren't so bad.'

'Oh and you know what'll really get their paisley-pattern bow ties twirling darling?' Veronica snapped, cutting her off. 'When I start talking about *that* film. *That* film. The one they all love to hear about. The one they all love to whisper about when I walk past them in the street or at a restaurant, or see me on some *classical* film channel. There she is. There is Veronica Lange. Whatever happened to her after *that* film? Decades of work before it, good work. Critically acclaimed work. And all they wanna hear is that. All they wanna hear is about how it absolutely ruined by life. How it ended me back up *here*.' She threw her arms out gesturing to the floor and then to Sue's now totally comatose body.

'They ruined it, not me' Veronica continued, but through the early stages of a cry. 'The director, the producers, the editors, the writers. I acted my heart out filming that and they turned into this cartoon piece of slap-stick trash. And *they* are the ones who laughed the most,' she said flinging her arms towards Sue again. 'These men. These men you are so obsessed with ruined it and now they want me to regurgitate it so they can laugh again and again. Night after night. But I won't do it. You can bring in whoever you want here to tell me that it's a masterpiece, but I won't listen. I won't do it.'

'Fine, ok!' Kirsten sighed, gesturing wildly to try and get her to calm down.

'I won't give in to this sadistic request to humiliate myself for their entertainment. If this show fails because of its integrity, *my* integrity, to keep it decent and respectable, then so be it!' Veronica collapsed against the wall, covering her face, sobbing.

'Jesus,' Kirsten said under her breath, rubbing her face with both her hands. She watched Veronica for a moment, half expecting her to slide her whole body down to the floor and coil herself into the foetal position. But instead she braced herself before peeling away from it and stood glaring down at Sue, breathing heavily. She raised her hands to her face again but stopped short of pressing them against her skin.

'I'm not going to cancel the whole production Veronica because of one bad night of sales, Ok? It's not just you that's going to affect. There's the crew, the theatre, me...'

'Write them all a cheque and be done with it.' She waved one hand dismissively in the air and then covered her face with the other again. She started inhaling in a way that sounded like she was trying to hold off more tears with each breath. Raising her head again, she took one final deep suck of air and stared at Kirsten through the mirror.

'I'm sorry to have dragged you into all this,' she said softly. Kirsten glared at her back saying nothing. 'Maybe you were too young to be taken on by someone like me. Cut this loose and move on.' She stood up and walked over to Sue's body and folded her arms while she peered down into her face. She sighed and closed her eyes. 'I'm done. Call the theatre. Call the producers. Write them a cheque. It'll be a clean cut. No one will be out of pocket. Except me of course.'

Kirsten sighed heavily and rubbed her face, pressing her fingers hard into her eyes. The pressure stung with a dull ache as she felt the muscles around her face clench before bright, dancing lights began appearing in the darkness behind her eyelids. After a moment she let her hands fall down by her side again and looked up at Veronica solemnly.

'If I make this call now Veronica, it's over,' she said sternly but with all the gentleness of a concerned parent. 'I don't want you waking up tomorrow and calling me, begging me, to retract any statements, because you were just having a moment. Once I do this, it's over, Ok? I mean it.' Veronica looked up, her face drawn and sunken. Small, erratic lines of eye makeup had slid down her cheeks in dark streaks, fading out as they ran out of liquid around the area of her jawline.

'Do it,' she said sniffing. 'It's done.'

Kirsten took in a deep, heavy breath, held it long and high in her chest before sighing loudly. 'Right,' she said through all the air leaving her mouth and turned to the door before disappearing quickly into the darkness of the bowels of the theatre.

Veronica walked over to her vanity and slid heavily down into her seat once again. She glanced over her shoulder to the door to watch it click shut properly before reaching over into her huge black handbag and slowly pulling out a small, gold Oscar statue. She held it under her face carefully, one hand in an open palm cradling its tiny head and shoulders with the other hand wrapped protectively around the circular base. 'So this was it,' she said sighing quietly, peering deep into its stoney, non-existent expression. 'This was your last chance, Veronica Lange...'

A loud snore from Sue's nostrils pierced the room sending her into a wince. She gripped the statue hard, closing her eyes tightly as another still loud but slightly less grating snore emerged. Slowly she opened her eyes again and glared down at the little gold man. 'Say goodbye to Hollywood,' she sung softly to it. 'Say goodbye my baby.' She closed her eyes again and sat the statue down on the vanity. 'Say, good bye, my baby...'

The words trailed off, as her lips slowly fell shut together and all the sound she could manage to produce was a soft, delicate hum of the tune that never seemed to escape passed her throat. Sue's guttural nose noises continued on behind her but Veronica's slow fall into a heavy, sad, day dream distanced them further and further before she could eventually, barely even hear them at all. But with one, particularly loud roar, her eyes bolted opened and the vague beginnings of the dream were sucked back quickly into the deep recesses of her mind once again.

The snap of the door made Veronica jump and almost drop the statue that she saw she was now gripping tightly with both hands. She looked up to see Kirsten breathing heavily, red and flustered with wet eyes and dewy skin.

'Ok, so,' she puffed, edging her way slowly back into the room. 'We might have a small problem.'

'What?' Veronica spat back, still trying to settle herself back from, her day dreaming.

'Front of house seems to have let in the people with tickets and they're already in their seats.'

'So?' Veronica shot back. 'Just tell them to leave.'

'I did,' Kirsten said sharply. 'I told them. I told them tonight was off and they should leave.'

'And?'

'Well I got the sound guys to make an announcement over the speakers first. But they weren't moving. One of the guys in the seats stood up and waved me down from the booth. So I walked over and stood in the aisle talking to them for a minute, and well...'

'Well what?'

'They're kinda pissed.'

Veronica turned around, her mouth slightly open now and her eyes pierced. 'Pissed? What do you mean *pissed*?'

'They kicked off a bit and are now refusing to leave. They say it's because they know that you're here and they want you to come out anyway...'

Veronica's shrill scream rattled through the small room, reverberated off the walls and returned back to smack them both in the ears once again. She curled her fingers and their long plastic nails into tense, terrifying claws and held them shaking over her face as the rest of her body rattled with the noise. Instantly, Sue's body leapt forward like some enormous vampire rising manically from its sleep, howling in fright before looking around totally stunned and dazed, as one of her wigs slid slowly off her head.

7:15pm

'Wait, what?' Sue cried out, as she sat there rubbing her fingers deep into her eyes, forgetting finally about the thick layer of makeup that sat on her face.

'It's done darling. The decision's been made. Not by me.' Veronica waved her hand dismissively at her as she sat hunched over completely her desk. 'By them.'

'Who?' Sue asked, tilting her head, securing her hair down with a pin she had already stacked in another part of her head.

'Nothing, nothing' Kirsten said, lurching forward, trying to muffle anything further from her. 'She means that we are going to have to post-pone the show tonight. There's just a few things we need to figure out before we continue. It's just for tonight though, don't worry.'

'That all happened just in that time I was asleep?'

Kirsten shuffled about nervously on her feet. 'Yes.'

'Is there anything I can do? Is it sales? The tickets or something?'

'Yes, it's the bloody tickets!' Veronica shouted with her face buried in her hands still.

'No, no,' Kirsten said, waving her whole body about in front of Veronica, as she lurched forward more. 'Sales are fine. It's just some boring stuff. Really nothing for you to worry about. Supplier agreements. Contracts. Honestly, it's fine.'

'If it's the tickets, I can make some calls? Do like a ring around and get some people to come tonight.'

'Well fuck, where was *that* an hour ago?' Veronica screamed into her hands.

Sue tilted her head to the side, back and forth to try and peer around Kirsten's tiny body as she swerved about trying to obscure any further comments from Veronica. She frowned and squinted before looking at Kirsten directly and then asking gently, 'Is everything ok?'

Veronica's head rose up slowly from her desk and looked at Sue through the mirror. 'No darling,' she sighed. 'It's not. Unfortunately what you appear to be witnessing here today is my apparently inevitable, but no less spectacular, descent into obscurity.' Sues eyes darted from Veronica's crumpled body up to Kirsten who was nervously watching Veronica, waiting again to pounce in front of her once more. 'This,' Veronica said, rising from the chair, gesturing down to her dress and then out across the room. 'Is all for nothing. I thought there was a spot left for me still in this world to be taken seriously. But all they seem to want to do is laugh.' She sighed heavily, before collapsing back into the vanity again.

Kirsten looked down at Sue and smiled awkwardly again, her eyes stressed and dilated. 'I think it might be best if we got you home now. Would you like me to call you a taxi or something?'

Sue leant forward on the couch and stood up to walk over to

Veronica. She paused when she arrived behind her and went to place a hand on her shoulder, but when she saw Kirsten shake her head nervously, she pulled back, placed it by her side and fell back into the couch again. Veronica looked up at them both through the mirror and sighed. 'I imagine you probably wish you never came now?'

'No, of course not.'

'Well, I'd suggest you go before you see anything else that might make you think otherwise...' She trailed off, hanging her head slowly.

'We can help fix it Ms Lange.'

Veronica locked her eyes on her instantly and leant into the mirror. She took a deep breath in through her nose and held it tightly. 'You can help fix it?'

'Yes.'

'You want to help fix *this*?'

'Yes, I can-'

The sharp slap of both her wide, open palms against the slick plastic of the table top violently rattled through the room and shook everything that laid around them on the surface. Kirsten twitched uncomfortably but Sue didn't move an inch. '*You* ruined it!' Veronica screamed. 'You can't help fix it,' Veronica continued. 'Because this is *your* damn fault, darling.'

'Whose fault?'

'You,' Veronica stabbed a finger into the mirror. 'You and all those men sitting out there now in the dark, clutching their tickets, refusing to leave, feeling so damn entitled to this performance, of trying to force me to laugh at myself for two hours. I won't do it.'

'What do you mean laugh? They're not laughing.'

'Oh aren't they darling? Check your phone. Check the comments.'

Sue shot a look of desperate confusion to Kirsten who frowned sympathetically, before looking to the floor for a moment and then back up to her. 'There's been some negative reviews.'

Sue nodded quickly, clasping her hands together tightly. 'But Ms Lange, I am not part of all that.'

'You're not?'

'No of course not.'

'And yet you come in here dressed up like this? Like some side-show, cattle station circus version of me. After you've pranced around your sweaty clubs all night mocking me, with your rubber chest and over drawn lips, and what? Am I supposed to be flattered by that?'

Sue didn't move. She clasped her hands tighter together across her stomach and just watched on. For a moment Kirsten thought she saw one of her long legs quiver underneath her gown, the sequins around the section of her knees twinkling slightly as if a small breeze had blown through her, glistening as whatever was making them move, shook gently behind them.

'I didn't think so,' Veronica said sighing. 'So, you can leave now and you can take all your friends out there with you when you do. This is over. Ok? It's done.'

Sue's broad, solid shoulders dropped slowly, curling towards her chest and then to the ground. She laid her her huge, soft hands over her lap, pausing briefly to steady herself and stood, glaring only at the ground as she did, saying nothing, taking slow, shallow breaths. She delicately plucked her handbag from the side of the couch and adjusted her dress. Veronica watched her for a moment before reaching over to open her cigarette case, placing one in her mouth loosely. As Sue stood again to move slowly toward the door, Kirsten leapt quickly over to her and placed a hand on the lower section of her back and softly edged along with her towards the door. She heard her sniff quickly twice behind her mass of hair, but she couldn't quite see her face to know if she was actually crying yet or not.

'Oh, and before you leave,' Veronica said, peering at them both through the haze of smoke, into the reflection of the mirror. Sue stopped immediately and snapped her neck back around, a faint smile of childish expectation flashing across her face. Veronica squinted at her, tapping a section of ash with the tip of her finger into the glass tray. 'Delete that hideous photo would you?'

For a brief moment, all three of them stood in a brutal silence; Veronica not letting her eyes drop from Sue through the mirror, Sue fixated right back on her and Kirsten going back and forth between them both. Kirsten couldn't quite seem to figure out how Sue might retaliate, despite her relative, outward calm. She was clearly, deeply devastated but still had the faint scent of rage emanating from somewhere within her. Veronica, in all her equally contained anger, seemed ready to keep going, smouldering at the mirror, piling up the insults quietly inside her mouth.

When Sue finally lurched forward, Kirsten flinched slightly before she realised all she was doing was adjusting the strap of her handbag over her shoulder. She stood eyeing Veronica up from the folds of her gown on the floor to the top of her wig, blinking slowly, before taking a deep breath and gliding silently towards the door. As she passed Kirsten, she managed a brief, strained smile of genuine but fleeting thanks, which Kirsten returned quickly, dipping her head to the ground as she did. She remained there until the sound of Sue's hard, heavy heels clicking against the vinyl floor trailed off around the corner and into the distance before the space was totally silent once again.

Closing the door slowly behind her and folding her arms, Kirsten stood focused on the boney, exposed curve of Veronica's open back, still not quite seeing her face clearly through the remaining smoke. She walked over till she was only a few feet from touching her, staring into the mirror. 'I realise you've made your mind up to tap out of this,' she said, folding her arms in tightly across her chest. 'But I don't think you need to scorch the earth behind you as you do.'

'Telling the truth scorching the earth now?' Veronica spat back quickly. For a moment the brutal silence returned again with Veronica glaring into nothing above her and Kirsten, standing with her arms folded and eyes focused on her. 'You know how many people told me I was mad to take you on?' Veronica mumbled. Kirsten felt her body tense up again. The backs of her teeth clamped down on each other and her chest tightened. 'What are you talking about?'

'She's too young,' Veronica said her voice heightening to mimic some absent person. 'She's not going to be able to handle you. She's inexperienced,' Veronica waved her hand dismissively. 'I personally didn't care you were Asian. They said that. Not me.'

'What?'

'I could have cared less about any of that. More than anything, you know what I wanted? I wanted a *woman*. One that I knew was going to get it. And I still think you do. I really do...'

'Get what?' Kirsten said, unfolding her arms and stepping back from the mirror slightly.

'What I needed to get this done. I needed a woman to help try and fix forty years of being managed only by men. Of having to take on work that did nothing but put me up there on the screen, as something to aspire to have sex with. I wanted someone who could help me get out of that. And I think you could have. Remember our first meeting together, darling? All those months ago. You were tense, I could tell. You said so little. Just sat there quietly listening as I talked, plucking away at your salad and sipping on sparkling water all afternoon. I don't blame you. Christ knows what you had heard about me before we actually met. The things people would say. Men, again, obviously. Producers, directors, writers. About being difficult to work with. About being demanding or hysterical. And suddenly there you were, just planted right in front of me. All of what? How old are you? Twenty-eight?'

Kirsten stayed silent.

'And there's me, rattling on about the future. My future. Our future. All this. You had these funny, interesting suggestions I remember, about starting with something on TV. Something small, you said. A cameo maybe on some show. Just to wet their appetite, you said. Ease myself back into things. Back into people's lives after being gone from the light for so long. You were being smart. But I wouldn't have it, would I? I wanted *this*. This, monstrosity we currently find ourselves in. For all my self indulgent rambling about going back to basics with something in a theatre. Something I needed to control from every possible angle. Did you walk away from that lunch darling, with a sense of just how burnt I had been by the world? By that film? By what they did to me after it? Did you admire my drive to turn those decades of being sidelined and forgotten into something practical? Or did you just think all my grand delusions were something you might be able to make some money from? I imagine the person you saw that day, so full of fire and lightening, is a far cry from the injured, lame cow you're seeing now. She was so formidable, so stupidly excited and aroused by her own ideas. I thought we were about to do something extraordinary here, but...' Veronica paused briefly looking down before folding her shoulders over the back of her chair and arching her throat up towards the ceiling. 'They wouldn't let us. Those men out there in the dark.'

She flopped herself forward towards the vanity again and held her face in her hands, her hair draped around her now like a tattered old shawl. Everything that had once before seemed so tall, so terrifying and intense about her to Kirsten, seemed to be seeping from her quickly. The black dress that had appeared to, so perfectly envelope and wrap her body, now swallowed her as it fell from her shoulders and gathered in unflattering folds around her bent waist and bare feet. The synthetic hair of her wigs, that had been positioned, pinned and sprayed up so high and beautiful, now caught slightly too much shine in the harsh light of the vanity lamps and eventually when she raised her head again to meet her own reflection face to face, the decades that lay behind her were suddenly wholly visible in the deep lines around her mouth and the sunken pockets of dark skin beneath her eyes. It was the first time since they met that Kirsten felt she saw Veronica look anything but totally in control of crafting her own image. The first time she had allowed herself to succumb to whatever way the world around her intended her to look.

After leaving her to settle in the moment, she sighed heavily, shuffled on her feet and then dropped her head to the floor. 'Let me go and see if I can reason with these guys in the audience again,' she said. 'I'll try clear them out with security and then I will head off myself.'

Veronica turned around, her eyes red and full with moisture and nodded gently. 'Thank you.'

'Are you going to be ok here for a moment?'

'Yes, I'll be fine.'

She kept her gaze on Veronica's back, half expecting her to collapse crying before she had even fully left the room. But she just sat there, staring into nothing.

As the click of the door sounded and the room was silent and empty once more, Veronica noticed one of the red lights on her desk phone begin to flash erratically. She squinted over at it, expecting the shrill ring to start echoing through the room, but it was silent, with only the light continuing to blink at her from underneath a small plastic label that someone had written the word 'reception' on in blue ink. She stared at it curiously for a moment longer before reaching for the receiver and placed it to her ear gently. 'Hello?'

'Ms Lange, I have your daughter Amy on the other line.'

'Who?' she spat back, choking on the word. The voice on the other end was silent for a moment, before repeating.

'Your daughter, Amy. Would you like me to put her through?'

Veronica didn't speak or move. Her shoulders pinned back and she held her breath. She slowly let the receiver drop to rest against her shoulder while she closed her eyes and took a deep inhale, careful to ensure it was silent enough to not be heard back through the phone. 'Who?' she said again mindlessly into the air around the phone, only to bide herself more time to comprehend the statement. The voice on the other end mumbled something back again, but she was so distant from the moment, even if she had had it screamed into her ear, it would have had the same effect. She closed her eyes tightly and placed a hand over the exposed skin of her chest and neck before taking in a deep, tense breath.

'Yes, hello,' she said, still half way through the exhale.

'Ms Lange would you like me to put her through?'

'Sure,' she said slowly. It clicked shut for a second and was silent before the white noise of a distant line of dense traffic filled the earpiece. 'Darling!' Veronica squealed with some previously undiscovered bout of energy.

'Hello Mother, darling.'

'Amy, darling, what a pleasant surprise.'

'How are you doing with everything down there? On stage again? What a riot.'

'Isn't it just?'

'And how does it feel?

'Like I never left darling.'

'I'm sure they missed you on Australia's Broadway.'

'Do they miss me in Hollywood?'

'Wailing, Mother. Wailing your name.'

'Stop it.'

'Wailing from the balcony of some hacienda in Brentwood, screaming, What's the matter Veronica Lange? Where did you go?'

'Oh stop it would you?' Veronica laughed nervously. 'Are you in Hollywood darling?'

'New York. Broadway.'

'Broadway indeed.'

'A press trip though, all work and so on…'

'Oh?'

'The film, you know?'

'Which film darling.'

'The new one. Didn't you see the article?'

'What article darling?'

'The Vanity Fair article?'

'Oh, no sorry darling. Far too busy opening the show. We are sold out. It was a riot.'

'I have a new film out. Next week.'

Veronica cleared her throat loudly, pausing before responding again. 'Oh, well how marvellous. What's it about?'

'Didn't you read the article?'

'No I just said that-'

'The journalist sort of caught me off guard. I'm sorry, I know you don't like being spoken about like that. It was just a question about your Oscar ceremony and then straight into mine. It's really nothing. Don't worry.'

'Truly haven't had a minute for anything, darling I'll try and read it soon. Terribly sorry.'

'People were tagging you online so I just thought you might have seen it.'

'Tagging?'

'On Twitter and whatnot.'

'Kirsten deals with all that. I never bother to look at any of it.'

'Well I just wanted to ask. You never know, it might be good for the show.'

'What do you mean?'

'People read it, start Googling you. See that you have something new on...'

'I don't think we need more press. Like I said, it's a full house.'

'It's Vanity Fair Mother...'

'Well good for you darling. I'm sure it's a wonderful piece. Whatever it's about.'

'The new film.'

'Oh yes, sorry. Quite right.'

'It comes out next week.'

'Ok,' Veronica paused for a moment, biting her bottom lip. 'That's lovely dear. I just, y'know the show and all. Busy and all that.'

'Any press for you guys then?'

'What press?'

'Press. Reviews. Press'

'Oh, umm, no, not yet.'

'Not yet? What time is it there? Must be after five? What's going on? Veronica Lange is on stage again for the first time in a century and there's no press? Can't be.'

'Well some press darling. But nothing of consequence.'

'What do you mean nothing of consequence?'

'You know, people on their phones and what not.'

'Twitter?'

'Yes and the rest...'

'Anything from anyone else though? The Guardian or even bloody TimeOut or something?'

'No, no...'

'You Sure? Honestly there must be something. Let me check for you now, one second…'

'No!' Veronica screamed, pressing the receiver into her mouth before reeling back again and trying her best to laugh it off again. 'No, it's fine, I already checked. Kirsten is on it, don't worry yourself. She is on it.'

Amy was silent with just the drone of the traffic coming through. Eventually she took a deep breath and spoke quickly through the exhale. 'Ok then. Well I just wanted to see how everything was going?'

Veronica leant into the mirror. She dabbed at her swollen eyes and the smears of mascara that now trailed out from them, the red gloss that had worn away from from the centre of her lips and now gathered at the edges of her mouth and the stressed droplets of moisture that lingered above her brow line. She glanced over to the door, wanting desperately to be interrupted so that she wouldn't have to answer the question. So that should could apologise, have to hang up quickly and disappear into the night. But there was nothing and no one to help. She took another deep breath in, and spoke as she exhaled.

'Oh darling it's marvellous, everything is going marvellously. Full house again tonight, another big party after planned. Great sales for the rest of the week. Just marvellous.'

'Full house?'

'Yes darling.'

'Tonight?'

'Yes, isn't that fabulous?'

'Yes I guess thats-'

'Such a thrill to be back on stage again. This is where is it all began right? Well for me anyway.'

'So you're sold out? Tonight?'

'Yes darling, isn't it marvellous.' Veronica began to feel her palms sweat between her skin and the plastic of the phone. She gripped it tighter and pressed it harder into her ear.

'Well, that's good news, I guess...'

'Tell me about this film then darling. What's it on?'

Another silence fell between them as Amy held her answer. Veronica felt herself breathing deeper into the speaker and pulled away from it slightly. She heard her daughter rustling gently on the other end and paused, suddenly concerned she had been talking too much. She waited desperately for her to respond, then for some indication she was about to sign off. To sigh and wrap up the rest of their awkward words with some hasty farewell and best wishes. She held the receiver away from her ear, suspending it in the space between her body and the cradle on the vanity, listening for a sign that it was all over. But the only thing coming through was the scratchings of the city in the background and Amy's pensive breaths. As she put it back to her face, she heard her take in a sharp breath and sigh heavily. 'You know Dad's come to see your show tonight?' she said in a tone Veronica had not heard before. She pulled the phone back slightly and looked into the receiver.

'He's what?'

'Dad there. At the theatre.'

'Tonight?'

'Yes, *tonight*.'

Veronica placed a hand over her chest. She pressed the air out through her pursed lips and clutched the phone tighter. 'I don't think so darling, he might have meant last night.'

'Well he just texted me before and said he's inside.'

'He's said he's here now? Inside the theatre?'

'Yeah, about half an hour ago.'

'Fuck,' Veronica bellowed out into the room, shoving one of her long finger nails between her teeth and biting down hard. She glared around the corners of the room, as if half expecting her ex-husband to appear from behind some of the furniture. Amy was silent again with the traffic noises finally starting to fade away as it appeared she had found the privacy of an alcove to stand in wherever she was. Several moments passed where it sounded like she went to speak, but would hesitate and simply mumble into the phone.

'And what else did he say then?' Veronica finally snapped back to her. 'With his texting.'

'What do you mean?'

'What else did he tell you after he arrived?'

'Nothing.'

'*Nothing*,' Veronica mocked her. 'So he didn't tell you he's sat out there now in an empty theatre?' Amy stayed quiet. 'He didn't tell you he's sat there now with not even thirty other people in that theatre, that now refuse to leave after we've cancelled it? He didn't tell you that the show's been eviscerated by nearly everyone's that's seen it?'

'No.'

'Oh bullshit he didn't!' Veronica screamed down the phone. 'He's told you and that's why you've called. He's called you from that mass of vacant chairs out there in the dark, laughing along with the rest of them as all this unfolds and because he can see it all about to burn down around him and then *you* called because you wanted confirmation straight from the source that it was all true.'

'Christ sake Mum. It's not -'

'Don't try and piss on my leg and tell me it's raining darling, I don't need your pity or your fathers or anyone's pity for any of this. None of this is my fault Ok? None of it. It's all their fault, you hear? Them. Out there.'

'Listen…'

'No *you* listen, Miss Vanity Fair. You call here and pretend like you want to chat, tip toeing around what you already knew was true. What did you expect I would say?'

She paused again, but Amy wasn't responding into the silence she was being offered. For a second Veronica expected her to hang up, to shove her phone back in her pocket, get back on with her day and forget about her and everything that was going on inside the tiny room. But she stayed there, connected, listening.

'Would you calm down?' Amy finally said. 'Why didn't you just tell me the truth when I asked instead of lying about it being sold out? I could have helped you.'

Veronica scoffed loudly and threw the handset down on the table with a crash. She paced away from it, hunched in the corner with her back to the mirrors, glaring down at the phone, pushing aggressive breaths through her nose and squinting. She heard Amy's voice trying to come through in frustrated bursts, attempting to draw her back to it, but she just stood there, waiting for the tone of the noise that would follow her hanging up. Finally one made it out, semi-audible though the handset. 'Mum!' it screamed.

Veronica dove towards the phone and crouched down, all but pressing her lips against its plastic surface. 'Darling shouldn't you be going? Don't you have some drag pageant to host or something?'

'What?' Amy shot back.

'Oh don't think I don't know how you work this.'

'What drag pageant?'

'You and your little friends in New York, playing dress up like Mummy Dearest, laughing and howling at me while I sit here, banished and exiled from the world.'

'What are you talking about?'

'You, in those bars. Judging some look-a-like contest about me. Amy, how do you think that makes me feel?'

'Oh, that. It just was a bit of fun, calm down. Dont-'

'But still you don't think twice about doing something that will leverage yourself, using *my* name, do you darling? Never have, this whole time. *Daughter of*, right? Never, just you. Never just you, as I had to do it. All of you, your father too, sucking every last bit of milage out of the brand Veronica Lange, while the body at the centre of it all slowly withers.'

Amy let out a sarcastic laugh directly into the phone, before sighing loudly. 'When you can't even fill a shitty, independent theatre in the fucking back streets of Sydney, exactly what doors do you think your name is opening these days for me, Mother?'

Veronica fell back from the phone and placed a hand over her mouth to muffle a panicked gasp. She turned away to face the mirrors, closed her eyes tightly and pulled her hair up from her neck with her other hand, frozen in the moment before she appeared as if she were about keel over completely and cry into her knees. But she was still. She took several short breaths in through her fingers, silently trying to steady herself. After a moment, she turned back to the phone, glaring down at it, the red light still glowing softly up at her, beckoning her back to the moment. She let it blink once more, before diving towards it, smashing the handset down into its cradle up and down, over and over.

'What the hell is going on?' Kirsten asked through a short exhale as she pushed through the door slowly. Both women glared manically at one another, stunned and briefly out of breath.

'Nothing. It doesn't matter,' Veronica said quickly, still with a hand pressed heavily on the phone, before shaking her head and placing her face into her open palms. 'What is happening out there? Did they leave?'

'Nothing happened. Well,' she placed her phone in her pocket. 'Something happened.'

'What?' Veronica shouted into her hands as they enveloped her face.

'You ex-husband is in the audience. He snuck in late.'

Veronica scoffed, looking up, but without opening her eyes. 'I know. Did he see you?'

'How did you know?'

'Amy called again. He's obviously told her what's going on, and she's called.' Veronica squinted towards her, folding her arms and pursing her lips. 'What was he wearing?'

'Like a blue safari suit I think? Why?'

'For god sake,' Veronica scoffed again. 'Why tonight?' she wailed, raising her arms towards the roof. 'Why?' She turned around and stomped towards the mirrors, pausing as she positioned herself almost pressing against them. 'So what did you tell them all? When will they go?'

'Ah, well...'

'What do they want? Is it money? Is that it? They want refunds? Here,' she lunged at her handbag and threw it on the floor so it's contents splayed across the carpet. 'Take it. Bloody take it!'

Kirsten stared at the tiny, mundane objects as they scattered themselves about Veronica's feet whilst she continued to walk around in small, panicked circles on the opposite side of the room. The worn sticks of make-up, credit cards, coins and tissues crunched under her heels as she mindlessly trod over and around them, crushing them into the plush pelt of the carpet beneath her. After a few circles, she paused and stood staring down at the floor with her arms folded and her back to the door.

Kirsten noticed the red light of the reception button flare up on Veronica's desk phone again, first once in a long, drawn out blink before it then started flashing like a siren. She thought for a minute to ignore it completely, but then fearing the person calling may be someone slightly too important to be on the receiving end of what would definitely be some manic tirade from her, should she see it, she silently approached it herself and gently pulled it up towards her face.

'Hello?' she said softly, bracing herself for Veronica's aggressive attention to rain down her. 'Um, no, it's not a good time.' She paused again to listen, this time for longer before holding her breath. 'Fine, I'll ask...' she trailed off, letting the receiver rest gently on her shoulder.

Veronica raised her head and glared over to her, demanding she elaborate without managing to say a single word. 'It's Danny,' Kirsten said gently, half preparing to have to put the phone back down immediately. She watched Veronica hunch herself over as if she was listening to someone scrape nails down a board. Her shoulders pulled up towards her ears and a brief shudder rolled down her back. Kirsten waited to simply hang up in lieu of what appeared to be Veronica's inability to even acknowledge what she had said. But just as she went to do so, she watched as in one seamless movement, she dove towards the phone, smashing several fingers at once against the loudspeaker button and stood back. Kirsten dropped the receiver and stood back.

'What Danny? What? What is it?' she screeched down into it.'What?'

'Von, honey. What's going on here?' his voice crackled through at her.

'What the hell do you think you are you doing? Why are you even here?'

'I wanted to see the bloody show. What do you mean, why am I here? Is this going to turn into one of your late appearance things? It's an old hack Von, people don't stand for that shit anymore.'

'Danny, tonight? Tonight, you wanted to see the show? Of *all* nights. Why? Where were you last night?'

'It was sold out! I couldn't get a ticket.'

Veronica leaned back and looked up towards Kirsten. 'Mr Showbiz himself, couldn't get a ticket?'

'Von, what is this?' he pleaded through the speaker. 'Why is this theatre so empty? There's barely fifty people here. And why aren't you on yet?'

'Danny just leave please and take your friends with you. The show is cancelled I won't be coming on. Goodbye.'

She slammed the handset down and the room was silent once

more. Leaning forward, she placed both hands on the table, her hair draping over her shoulders and her back muscles rising and falling quickly with her deep breaths. 'I can't take much more of this,' she said behind the curtain of her cascading wig. She tilted her head up slightly, her eyes barely visible through the thick curly ringlets. 'I need to leave.'

She pushed herself up and glared down at the contents of her purse still splayed about at her feet, before slowly crouching down on her knees and with broad sweeps of her arms, started to pile the items back together. Still not quite seeing her face, Kirsten began hearing the faint sound of her sobs and realised she was now actually crying. The past hour or so, she had managed to just appear as if she was on the brink of tears, but finally they were being allowed to fall from her in between quiet, childish weeps.

Without even thinking Kirsten found herself falling to the ground slowly also, first onto her knees and then to her hands, plucking bits of human detritus from between the thick fabric hairs of the rug. Veronica didn't look up. She was focused on her own corner, scratching at the objects and placing them slowly back into the large leather bag beside her.

They stayed on the floor together for some time, hunched over, not talking, moving quietly about like two old gardeners tugging at weeds. At one point Kirsten found herself just staring into the long white hair of the carpet, watching it as it grew up around the fingers of her open palms, listening to Veronica scurrying away behind her. A brief thought flashed through her that this chaotic moment spent on the ground together, might just be the last time she ever saw her. That Veronica, in all her shameless, self indulgence, would have no problems whatsoever disappearing from the world entirely. No problems retreating back into some sort of grand solitude, ageing in total isolation, inside a large dark house, heavily perfumed in rose water, completely quaffed and draped in silk dressing gowns, midday drunk on sweet imported wine, smoking whilst creating fantastic stories about how the world would be talking about her still, about how it would be pining for her the longer she remains hidden and the more fantastic the lies about where she was and what she was doing would become, all the while people screaming from the streets, What's the matter Veronica Lange? Where did you go?

An anxious knock at the door of the dressing room saw both women bolt to their knees like two annoyed meerkats. They shot brief, concerned looks at one another and then back at the door again, before a second knock sounded. Eventually Danny's long, skinny silhouette emerged slowly from behind it as he pushed through the entrance with no absolutely consideration for what was happening on the other side of it.

The first thing Kirsten found herself staring at was just how implausibly black his hair now seemed under the harsh lamp light of the dressing room; their bright yellow glow seemingly sucked directly into it like some lifeless void. It was a black that was verging on impossible for a man of his age and made his hair seem less like a part of his body and more like an item of clothing that he put on each morning. He was stitched into a figure hugging, double breasted, navy blue, safari suit that flared wide opened at the chest with the collar of the pristine white shirt underneath sitting so high and structured it scraped the bottom of his jaw. He wore a collection of small gold rings across multiple fingers and a thin gold chain that slung loosely over a perfectly smooth, slightly too tanned chest. A thick musky cologne seemed to linger around him in a haze that penetrated through any other scent that might be present, burning the nose and stinging the eyes.

'Sweetheart,' he shouted down towards the floor where Veronica knelt still. 'What's all this then? Jesus it's warm in here. And Veronica Lange on the floor? C'mon, get up. Those fairies won't wait much longer for you out there.' He quickly cocked his head to look beside her. 'How ya doin' Kirsten? Good?'

Veronica placed a hand on the side of the lounge and braced herself as she rose. Kirsten watched her silently, not moving to help but tense at the prospect of having to dive towards her should she fall. Once she was fully upright, she folded her arms tightly across her body and squinted across the room towards him, sighing. 'Danny, please just go home.'

'Von, what is going on? You're booked here for three weeks and you're tapping out for the second night?'

'I'm tapping out completely. It's done. I've cancelled it all.'

'Why though?'

'*Why*? It's none of your business why Danny. You can't just storm in here acting like you work here again.' she said gesturing to her room. 'Please just leave, would you?' She walked over to her vanity and stood hovering over it, mumbling to herself. 'Of all fucking nights to come...'

Kirsten edged up beside Danny, leaning in closely and dropped her voice. 'We're trying to get everyone out of the theatre but it doesn't seem to be working.'

'I've noticed.'

'You included!' Veronica shouted, from the vanity, not even bothering to turn around. Kirsten rattled her head, closed her eyes briefly and then looked up again at Danny.

'Maybe you could help?' Kirsten said gently to him.

'How?'

'Come out with me again and try speaking to these guys. It was getting tense last time I went out. I just don't want it escalating further and for people to start putting it all on Twitter or anything. Would you mind?'

She stood back and watched as one of Danny's dark eyebrows rose slowly and his lips turned upright into a slight wince. He folded his arms and took a deep breath, looking down at Kirsten. 'What a fucking mess,' he said back at her, not nearly quiet enough to prevent Veronica from hearing. Kirsten shot him a strained smile and nodded slowly. She watched as his eyes shot up briefly and he began glaring over her to Veronica's now totally slumped body at the vanity. He frowned, pausing for a moment before taking two giant strides that ensured he arrived instantly behind her. He placed both his hands on her shoulders and leant down towards her ear. 'What's the matter, Veronica Lange? What's happened?' She looked up slowly into his reflection through the mirror. Her eyes were red and swollen, the under sections inflated and glistening with moisture. 'Talk to me,' he said gently.

Veronica tilted her head up to face him in the mirror and locked his eyes. For a moment it seemed like she would ignore his plea, face herself back to the table and fall into some deep day dream. But when she saw him standing there, she sighed gently and let her shoulders slouch. 'I don't even know how this all happened,' she moaned. 'I just…'

'Tell me honey.'

'Last night, everyone was here. The seats were full, they were clapping. I got a standing ovation. A big one. You should have seen it. The whole theatre on its feet. There was a party. A huge party after. Everything was fine...'

'And now what?'

'Well Christ, Danny, you've been out there. You've seen it. That.'

'There no one there...'

As Veronica mumbled through her own version of what was currently unfolding, Kirsten felt her phone vibrating against her thigh and discreetly turned her back to them to open it. There were two missed calls from front of house and a message that after she flicked the screen open she began mouthing quietly to herself as her eyes scanned it. There is a bunch of guys out the front, wanting to buy tickets, it read. What do I do?

Kirsten pulled the phone closer to her face. If they're paying, she tapped out quickly, Let them in. She watched as the bubbles of an impending response appeared, pulsating with the prospective text. Is she actually going on stage though? it shot back. Kirsten pulled her phone even closer, typing only with her thumbs. Just get them inside...

'... and the way they speak about me on the internet Danny, if only you could see it.'

Kirsten looked up to see Veronica glaring at her ex-husband longingly from the chair, sunken deep into it, both his hands planted firmly on her slender, slouching shoulders. 'It's just vile, these people and what they say about the show.'

She paused and took a deep breath to stave off another long cry, but just before she could speak again another loud, heavy knock came through the other side of the door. A split second of stressed silence fell between the group again, each one of them shooting confused and concerned glances at one another, before the sound of the handle clicking down came straight after. Kirsten bolted over to it and placed her hand flat on her side of the door, trying to stop it from being pushed in any further, but the gentle force surged her body inward and even with it only half open, it was instantly obvious who it was.

'Guys, it's just me again,' Sue's deep, nervous voice rolled through the air.

'Oh fuck me,' Veronica howled and slammed her face down across her folded forearms.

'I think I've left my keys behind, I'm so sorry,' Sue said as Kirsten opened the door slightly further. 'Could I come look quickly?'

Kirsten tried her best to smile up at her as she twisted the leather handle of her handbag tightly in both hands, shooting stressed looks over her shoulder at Veronica.'Umm,' Kirsten mumbled, darting back and forth to Sue and then over to Veronica again, before leaning into the gap of the door and whispering. 'I don't think this is a good time.'

'I know,' Sue leant into Kirsten's face, whispering hard also. 'I just can't get into my flat, can I?'

Kirsten sighed heavily and rubbed her face. 'Ok, just stay here I'll look for you,' she said, leaving the doorway and diving into the couch, shoving her hands behind the cushions manically. She turned back to her to offer a reassuring smile through the small crack she left in it, but watched in horror as it creaked slowly open, exposing Sue's dazzling body to everyone inside once again.

'What have we got here then?' Danny's gravelly voice rattled through what was about to be another tense silence. 'A real life show girl, huh?'

Sue smiled down at him politely, flicking a large lock of her wig to one side to better see the source of the comment. She seemed briefly too concerned with assessing his outfit to even respond.

'Danny Shields,' he said sticking a long arm out over the floor between them as he lunged towards her. Sue shot him a faint grin, but let her hand dangle in the air, gesturing for Danny to only hold it gently, not shake it.

'Sue,' she mumbled.

'Ignore him,' Veronica scoffed from the vanity.

'What brings you here of all places darling? Are you in the show?'

'No, she's not.' Veronica mumbled.

'I was gonna say,' Danny laughed, standing back to better examine Sue. 'Von, that's *very* modern of you.'

'No,' Sue said, sounding sad. 'I was here before. I've just left something behind. I'm sorry to interrupt.'

'No, don't be silly. Stay. We are having a bit of a crisis talk anyway. Maybe you could help?'

'Sorry, I don't mean to be rude, but who are you?'

Danny cackled again, this time in a piercingly higher tone forcing Veronica to cower down further into her chair. 'The old guard sweetheart,' he said placing his hands into both the pockets of his trousers. '*Mr* Veronica Lange.' Sue shot a confused look towards Kirsten, who smiled awkwardly and nodded.

'Oh! Right. Ok,' she smiled nervously. 'Of course. Hello…'

'So what can we do for you darling huh? What's brought you into the dragon's den?'

'I just need my keys.'

'Right well, this way please. Come, you may as well take a seat while we sort it all out for you. A drink also perhaps?' Danny gestured theatrically with his arm out towards the couch, while he scanned the small space for any sign of a bar, but Sue didn't move from the door. When he came back to her still standing frozen in the frame he sighed. 'Right, well. As you wish.' Kirsten dove into the couch again, fumbling in the cushions for Sue's keys. 'So,' Danny continued with all the forced enthusiasm of a bored circus ringleader. 'How did you two meet then?'

'Danny drop it would you? It's not important,' Veronica said.

'A seven foot tall tall drag queen swans into your dressing room Von, dressed like a spitting image of you and you expect me to just drop it?'

'Yes.'

'Absolutely not. So-'

Veronica shot up from her chair, pushing it into Danny's long legs behind her, sending him into a painful jackknife. All three looked to her frowning slightly as she towered in the space. Danny appeared to shrink several feet, edging back from her.

Veronica's body didn't move at all aside from the gentle nodding of her head as she appeared to be processing every word she was about to spit out. She poured a menacing glare down on Danny before closing her eyes and taking a frustrated inhale. 'I am going to go,' she said finally, in a low, deep scowl. 'I am going to go to the bathroom to fix myself up. I am going to come back to collect my things, and when I do, I want each and everyone one of you out of this room. And then I'm going to leave. Is that clear?'

No one spoke. She had asked the question, but it clearly had no room for interpretation or any sort of response. They all stood watching her, Danny fidgeting with his jacket nervously, Sue still wringing the strap of her handbag and Kirsten with her hands in the cushions. After silently assessing that everyone had properly comprehended what she had said, she turned and snatched a small make-up bag from a corner of the desk and shoved it under her arm.

'Christ sake Von, c'mon, where are you even gonna go?' Danny pleaded. She stopped dead in the doorway and straightened her back and neck before turning slowly.

'Danny what is it exactly that you suddenly seem to care so much about with this?' she said, throwing the small bag down on the bench again. 'What do you care if this shuts down or not? How does this affect you in *any* way?'

He shot a stressed glance over to Kirsten briefly. Veronica clocked it, looking at her also but then fixing her eyes back on him. 'It doesn't,' he said nervously.

'Exactly. So stay out of it. You've been out of this game far too long,' she said turning to grab at her things again. 'You wouldn't know anything about it anymore. Your time's passed. That's why I have Kirsten.'

Danny watched her for a second more, beginning to ready herself to leave again, before looking over at Kirsten. She noticed immediately his expression had dropped. 'Don't know anything about it?' he said softly as Veronica wafted passed him. She turned as he said it, folded her arms, pursed her lips and paused. 'Forty years in the business, is nothing is it Von? Well fuck me...' Veronica sighed, rolling her eyes. 'Getting you twenty odd starring roles,' he continued, 'Ten million a film. Two Academy Awards. What was that?'

'I see a nerve has been touched,' Veronica smirked, turning to Kirsten and Sue.

'You pluck this kid from no where and lump her with the task of bringing you back out of the shadows and but then have the nerve to tell me I don't know anything about it after forty-years?'

'Forty years *in* the business,' Veronica mocked him. 'You acted in those films did you sweet heart? That was you up there on the screen was it? See,' she said turning to the other two again and gesturing to Danny. 'This is what happens when you spend your life working in the margins of greatness, five feet from stardom. You can only bask in the scent of success, not the blinding beam of its lights. But it's just as intoxicating isn't it, darling? Just as consuming as being directly in the firing line of its lasers.'

'And what is this now, huh?' Danny said. 'All this success, has got you what? A half filled theatre full of old faggots who are only here to listen you talk about things you did thirty years ago?'

Kirsten felt Sue inflate somewhat next to her, but she didn't move. She just cleared her throat and folded her arms. 'I guess I have you to thank for that, don't I? You and all your fine publicity work on that film,' Veronica said.

'Well baby, like you said, it's you up there on screen isn't it? Not me.'

Veronica smiled sarcastically and laughed. 'Thank god for that.'

'And what is this whole performance about you and these guys out there, huh?' Danny waved an arm outwards the corridor.

'What performance?'

'Pretending like that theatre being filled only with fags has come as some fucking surprise to you.'

'I never said I was-'

'Maybe if you paid just a bit more attention over the years' he said, cutting her off, 'none of this would have come as such a shock. Because I tell you now Von, your fans have always only ever been gays. You've just never paid attention to it.'

'That's absolutely not true.'

'And how would you have ever even known that?'

'I know who my fans are.'

'You don't. Because you're were too busy banging on about being an artist, about art, about acting like it's some great cure to the shit of the world, that you stopped paying attention to the fact that when *they* stop paying attention to you, the moment they switch off that TV and turn away, none of what you do matters.'

Veronica folded her arms tightly across her chest and straightened her shoulders. Her eyes were darting up and down Danny's body back and forth, landing briefly on his face before dropping again. He glared back at her, unaffected. 'These guys out there in the dark tonight, all they want to do is be entertained. So if that means you going out there in a fucking beehive and a ball gown, crying about your shitty life, you go out and do it.'

Danny eyed Veronica up and down slowly once more and held his breath. He folded his arms and glanced across at Kirsten and then back to her again. 'I'm leaving,' Veronica said quietly. 'Please be gone by the time I am back. All of you.'

At first Danny didn't move, he just folded his arms and scoffed, smirking at her, silently prodding her to retaliate. But when he turned to face Sue, he realised he was face to face with something slightly more formidable than his ex-wife. He shuddered at her, unfolding his arm and puffed out his chest a little. Turning back to Veronica, offering her one last grimace, before she snatched her things from the table again and bolted out the door.

With just enough time to let her disappear from ear shot, Danny clapped his hands together gently and turned to face the others. 'Well, seems the party's over folks. Best clear out then before the cheque comes. Is there anything to drink in here?' He turned to face the other two but stopped as he saw the looks on both their faces glaring back at him as he did. 'Oh don't be like that,' he said sounding annoyed. 'She'll be fine. She's tough.'

Sue folded her arms and looked him up and down fully once before pursing her lips and looking away, sighing. 'Let me grab these keys and I'll be on my way,' she said bending into the couch. Danny stood back examining her, eyeing up her long body and shimmering dress as it twisted and moved while she dove behind the cushions.

'You're a queer lot aren't you?' he said finally with a smirk, focused on her shoes.

'I beg your pardon?' Sue said, straightening herself and turning to face him.

'I mean, we give you everything you want and you still complain.'

'What are you talking about?'

Danny laughed and pulled out a cigarette from a packet tucked inside his jacket and sparked it. 'You darling. You and those men out there in the dark. What is it you want after all?' Sue quietly folded her arms and inhaled deeply through her nostrils. 'You want Old Hollywood razzle dazzle?' Danny spoke through a breath of smoke. 'You want sequins and gossip and fairy floss. We give it to you and you still don't fucking show up to the party. Or, show you up and then complain that it's what? What did those reviews say?' He turned to Kirsten who quickly looked away. 'I mean, isn't that the fucking point?'

Sue bent over and gently plucked her keys from a crevice in between two pillows of the couch, placed them in her bag and clasped her hands together slowly. 'Us lot?' she said sighing heavily. 'You mean the ones actually paying to see this?'

'I mean...' Danny laughed and gestured out the door into the theatre.

'The ones keeping people like you working well passed your used by date?'

Danny laughed again and took a short drag, squinting into the residual haze. 'Us lot are the ones keeping the light of our idols alive even when the world, *your* world, casts them aside. We keep them alive when you say they're too old, too washed up, too temperamental. Not just for money like you do. Not for business. But because we love them. And because they mean something to us that people like you will never know. I know Veronica seems to think we are all incapable of telling the difference between real life and fantasy but what choice do we have? This,' she said gesturing around her to Veronica's racks of costumes and cluttered, make-up strewn vanity, 'is sometimes all we have. And if she can't appreciate the huge, delicate responsibility she has, if she can't handle a few hysterical requests to sign something at a restaurant or take a fucking photo in the street, well, then,' Sue paused and looked Danny up and down once, from his shoes to the top of his head. 'She doesn't deserve our love. And you don't deserve our fucking money.'

Veronica shoved the door open forcefully with the excess fabric of her dress falling from her hands as she stopped dead in the door. 'Why are you still here?'

'We're going. Calm down,' Danny said abruptly. He turned to the vanity and pressed the remainder of his cigarette into Veronica's glass ash tray before leaning into the mirror, flattening his blazer, and and then straightening his back again. 'Not sure what you're gonna do about those angry queens out there though sweet heart, but if anyone knows how to handle them, it's you. Best of luck.'

Danny smiled menacingly and blew Veronica a sarcastic kiss as he passed her. Just as he was about to fully disappear behind the door, he paused. 'Next time you feel like getting yourself back out there Von, call me to handle it. Not the kid, Ok?'

Veronica cackled loudly, right into Danny's face as he passed her. He stopped and turned to glare. 'Danny the last thing you handled for me, landed me back here. So I think I will be sticking with the *kids*, from now on.'

'Oh really?'

'Yes.'

'Well if she's so amazingly adept at doing all of this, why is she paying me on the side for advice on how to handle this?'

Veronica glared over at Kirsten before blinking quickly and focusing back to him. 'She's not.'

'Isn't she'

'No,' Veronica spat back him, staring intensely at Kirsten again as she did.

'Right, then well, what were all those little clandestine coffee catch ups for, the last six weeks to try and plan how to promote it, hmm?' He splayed open his arms to Veronica and then to Kirsten. Veronica and Sue both turned to Kirsten also who had now shrunk herself into one of the far corners of the room. Sue edged away from her and glared down at her tiny frame, shuffling alone. 'She's no publicity prodigy and it's not just a coincidence that this theatre is full of queers, Von. We did that. Her and I. Together.'

'What are you talking about?'

'Me Von. It was my idea. All of this. To have the posters for this plastered all over the cloak rooms, toilet doors and above the filthy urinals of their night clubs and saunas and fucking STI clinics. To hand stacks of free tickets to drag queens to dole out to the drunk crowds of their shows. My idea. But we did it. *Together*. Me and the kid. Isn't that right honey?' He said menacingly towards Kirsten. 'Because Von that's all that was going to work. That is all that was going to work to get you back here. Hundred bucks a ticket, who do you think was going to pay that beside those men out there in the dark? No one. So that's what we did. And for a minute, it worked. For a minute, they ate it up. All you had to do was go up there and keep fucking singing honey but you couldn't even manage that. You couldn't even do that without falling into your own self pity about art and integrity again. Just give it up. Give it up and go out and fucking dance for the peanuts like you're supposed to.'

The crash of Veronica's heavy glass ashtray exploding against the wall behind him sounded before anyone even seemed to realise she had swept it off the vanity. It splintered into a thousand pieces of thick crystal, crushed butts and black, delicate ash against the brick, sending Kirsten and Danny cowering towards each other, whilst watching the mass of shards shower to the floor around them.

As she stood there, silently examining the scene, with her chin tilted high and her eyes bearing down, Veronica, let her arms drop by her side, dangling limp and scratching against the harsh fabric of her dress. The skin on her face was now layered in a fine mist of perspiration and the new black drips of eye make up that had rolled slowly through the thick foundation she had just reapplied to her cheeks shimmered in the lights from her mirror. She breathed slowly in and out an open mouth with her snarled, red, lips curled up and her teeth fully bared. Her already sharp collar bones had risen through the skin of her chest as her shoulders grew and fell in time with each breath.

Rising slowly from the corner, Danny scoffed and smiled as he examined the mess that he now stood in. He tauntingly kicked one of the larger pieces of glass back towards Veronica. 'Grow up,' he said, flicking some ash off his shoulder and lapel before disappearing out the door and into the darkness of the theatre's backstage tunnels.

Sue glared down to Kirsten who was completely hunched over herself, arms folded tightly across her front and head bowed towards her feet. She wasn't moving, wasn't speaking and barely even appeared to be showing any signs of life, aside from whatever residual strength was holding her upright still. She sighed heavily towards her, shaking her head as she did turning briefly to Veronica who she saw had fallen against the wall slightly and was bracing herself with an outstretched arm, holding her face in an open palm. She wasn't sobbing but her breaths were short and panicked still. Her body quivered with the adrenaline the fight had caused, almost totally overwhelmed by it. The tiny, mundane room, built only for the purpose of housing one, possibly two people at a time, for the putting on of some make-up or the quick change of an outfit, was suddenly filled with an entire cosmos of sadness and stress.

Veronica let her hand drop by her side and looked directly into Sue's eye's. Kirsten lifted her head slightly, just enough to catch the gaze also and for a fleeting moment, there seemed to be a brief, albeit silent, acknowledgement that each of them was hurting at about the same level of anguish. That there might just be a moment of brief tranquility to allow each of them to walk off, unscathed.

But just when Kirsten went to move first, a deep thumping noise began to emanate from outside the room. It bounced around the walls, rattling tiny, poorly secured objects from their positions and thudding deep within their ears as it seeped through the brick and windows like the distant booming of bass coming from a loud speaker across the street. It sounded over and over, chaotic and out of time, stopping briefly and then erupting once again. All three of them stood with their necks craned slightly towards the ceiling, angling their faces around to try and locate the source of it. They shot, brief confused glanccs at one another before returning their stares to the empty space above them. Eventually Kirsten went over to the small window with the opaque glass to the side of the room and leant her ear closer into the space. She shrugged when it was obvious the noise was no louder there than where she had stood before and returned to the entrance.

As she did, a great screech came charging down the corridor and through into the room; a long, chaotic cackle of voices, claps and whistles all echoing through the hallways, to accompany the thuds, pouring in around them as they stood there, stunned, shocked into silence, entirely ignorant still of what it might all be about.

Until they heard the first boo. Then the second. Then the third.

The third came in a great chorus that seemed to join up all the noises together; the stomps, the claps, the whistles and the cheers, followed by a deep, low hum of a group of voices all howling in frustrations at once. As the noises trailed off finally, appearing to tire of the harsh song they had begun, or pausing to get more air to continue, the stomps and claps continued on.

'It's those men in the audience,' Veronica said, finally breaking the stunned silence that had descended between them whist glaring around the ceiling. 'They're the ones making those noises. Those men from the theatre. Those men sat out there in the dark.'

Finally her eyes locked with Kirsten and Sue's, wide and desperate, wet and red with stress and pain. Strands of her wig hair now stuck to the moisture on her face. When a particularly loud thud came from the roof, she cowered slightly, ducking as if she felt the person responsible for it might fall through at any moment. Slowly she tilted her face back down to glare again towards Kirsten. 'They're booing me,' she said softly. 'The noises they're making. They're at me. They're booing at me.'

Kirsten took a deep inhale and felt her cheeks start to glow with heat and her hands begin to sweat. She looked quickly up at Sue who was staring at her feet, shuffling back and forth, clearly desperate to remove herself from not only the room but the situation. 'Veronica ,' Kirsten said softly. 'I'm sorry but-'

Another thunderous round of stomps, whistles and screams roared from the corridor into the room, cutting her off. It continued, rattling round the small space, pounding down from the ceiling and reverberating between the mirrors.

Just as Kirsten went to finish, she saw Veronica spin around with all the precision and speed of a young cat pouncing towards a rat and dive towards her Oscar on vanity. She held it by the neck, staring down at it manically, shaking in full, unbridled rage. Sue edged slowly more towards the doorframe, bracing herself for another missile from the other side of the room, but Veronica was still in her position, shaking but not moving otherwise. She squeezed another hand around the based of the statue and strangled it, forcing the blood in her fingers to drain and the flesh to turn a deathly white. Her teeth ground together and her eyes were squinted down into the blank face of the small gold man. She remained there, twitching, sweating and grinding, until it seemed she may collapse, fall to the ground in exhaustion and curl into a deep sleep, but after a moment, she simply sighed. She let one hand go limp by her side and the other with the statue follow shortly after. Her head dipped as she took another breath before looking up to meet her own reflection in the three long mirrors that stood leant against the walls of the room. Three versions of herself, all identical. Three times the sweat, three times the ruined make up, blotched cheeks and crooked wigs. Three disheveled gowns and three tortured Oscar statues. Three times the vision and three times the pain.

Another thud from the roof sounded, sending Veronica cowering towards the floor once again. Just one stomp though. Not the running or smashing of feet multiple times, just one loud bang. A thud so loud, it could almost only be from someone who knew she was there, right beneath them under her feet. Kirsten winced at the reaction she thought she new was coming. A scream, a smashed mirror, upended furniture, a vanity swiped of its contents with the wave of an arm. But there was nothing. For the moment, only the kind of silence that lingers after a disaster. A silence, with just hot air emanating from Veronica as she stood there hunched over, clutching the statue, sweating, glaring at herself. But before anyone else there could move, or even contemplate to move, to leave, to approach her to do anything, just like that, she was gone. Through the door and into the darkened bowels of the theatre.

Kirsten and Sue, both stunned into a dumb silence, glared idiotically at each other before Sue leant out the door to catch the fleeting glimpse of Veronica's sequins disappearing around the corner and out into the darkness of the stage. She returned to face Kirsten with a wide open mouth, looking from the vacant space between the mirrors and then back at her again with the only sign that Veronica was ever there with them to begin with, being the now lingering smell of her gardenia laden perfume and stale cigarettes.

Curtain

'Well,' Veronica shouted from the shadows of the wings. 'Here I am!' The stomps and whistles coming from the black mass of the seating area died the instant she spoke, with a confused quiet descending upon it right after. Only the sound of the back of her stilettos smacking the wooden boards filled the space as she marched out from the right of the stage and straight into the spotlight, the sequins of her dress twinkling manically as the beam drenched itself over them. The moment she came into full view, a collective gasp rose from the seats, followed by loud, inaudible murmurs and shocked, awkward laughs with the tiny, piercing white lights of dozens of phones all switched to record, flaring up soon after.

As she arrived slightly too close to the front of the stage, the few seating sections she could make out beneath her appeared peppered with bodies clustered in small groups of threes and fours. They huddled closely, leaning in to whisper to each other as she bore down on them from above, eyes open and expectant with frightened excitement. Behind them, shadowy outlines of more bodies moved and twitched in the seats also but in larger, more concentrated clumps. There was no way to tell precisely how many there were from where she was standing, but from what she could see, at least half the seating area in the theatre was taken up now. The only individual she could actually make out properly was positioned at one of the doors, appearing to have gone to leave before she arrived, but who now stood frozen, glaring down at her, partly illuminated by a green exit sign. She scanned the sea of people once more from the back of the dress circle, right to the very front rows again beneath her and then looked directly into the spotlight.

'So is this what you all wanted?' she asked, holding her arms out wide and with her Oscar dangling loosely from her hand. 'Is this what you were all crying out for? Why you are all refusing to leave as we asked you politely to do?' She edged slightly closer to the font of the stage, placing her free hand over her forehead to try and block the light from her eyes. 'Is this all you needed? Me to come out here like this and stand here for you?'

Nothing but silence came back to her; a dark, tense silence from a sea of people who only minutes before had managed to smoke her out of her room with their noise and chaos. She scanned the crowd again, her eyes starting to adjust to the black slightly better now. 'Quite the crowd in the end tonight, weren't we? All fire and fury just before, but now...' said raising her arms up and out, before letting them fall back by her sides again. 'Is this spill over from last night, or have you all just come for round two of the circus? The one where I stand here rotating like a broken ballerina having pennies flung at me while you write your nasty comments on your phones?'

She scanned the seats again with her palm above her eyes sighing, rubbing her free hand over her chest and across her shoulder. 'For the record,' she said projecting her voice still but looking down to the floor. 'For the record, I am well aware how this is all supposed to work. We're supposed to get along famously, aren't we? You and I. People like me, up here like this, and people like you out there in the dark. I am well aware that on the surface of it all, we are supposed to bask happily in the glow of our mutual love for each other. The other women like me, and you, these adoring, passionate, hysterical things that you are, with those big, wide eyes you all have glistening out from the dark, up towards us here and on your screens. Your idols and icons, the characters from all the worlds of your childish dreams and fantasies. All those stories that you felt like you actually lived in, so intensely and passionately, huddled under blankets, in front of the television, locked away in your rooms, dreaming yourselves out of your simple circumstances. I am aware of that responsibility we up here have. As keepers of those dreams and I'm aware of how this is supposed to look now. I know you want to love me. I can see that. But I know also,' she paused looking up finally and extending a finger out briefly towards the light. 'You still need me to fail too, don't you? You need to see in me a deep failure and unbearable sadness as I stand here in my long, expensive dresses, twinkling under these lights, dancing for you. You need to hear that scratchy, longing in my voice for all the love that I lost along the way to where I am now. For the all the harsh disappointments and piercing anguish that this fame has brought me. You need to hear in my voice a longing for the stability and calm that you know I can't have because of the fame. And in amongst all of that, you need to see me only get that love from you as I stand here. That yearning for love and acceptance, nourished only by the sight of you all sat out there in the dark. By your cheers and applause. I know that's how this is all supposed to work. You still need to see me fail to love me properly. To fall once and then again, get back up, dusty and wounded but still sparkling under these lights. To be beaten down by life and by fame but still drag myself out on stage to perform. Because we are supposed to fail together, you and I, aren't we? We are supposed to have this one thing in common. This expectation of failure, from being born on the sidelines of life. We are expected to understand suffering as equals, aren't we? And when you see me up here, you have to be able to see the suffering you see in yourself. When I fall, when the failures consume me and you see me tarnished by my work, chewed up and spat out by the system that made me who I am today, you can relate to being chewed up and spat out by the system that made you. We were brought up to be ordinary people in an ordinary world. We were raised to serve that together, as simple, normal, ordinary people but then what? We became extraordinary. We were both born, totally saturated in the ordinary but deep down inside we knew were weren't. And when I am up here, on stage, under these lights, in these gowns and diamonds I become this dazzling beacon of hope for you. Flamboyant, beautiful and unattainable success in the face of the adversity of your life. And you still need to see me fail, because you need to see that we are still in it together. But you won't see me fail. Because I might have taken you out of those difficult childhoods you had, replacing aggressive, unaccepting parents, punishing insensitive friends or teachers at your schools. I might have yanked you from your suburban obscurity up to the stage with me to bask in the light of the fame and adoration of this fantasy that I projected to you, in these things you watch, huddled under that blanket in front of that television, daydreaming, but I won't fail as you need me to. I won't. I won't be defined by the failures of my life. Of that film and what the world did to me after it. I know how this is supposed to work. You need to see me fail, to see in me here, on stage, in my life, the cost of that failure. Of the heartbreak and debilitating loneliness that comes with it. And to feel the acceptance and support I need to keep going, coming only from you, out there in the dark. But for all the power and might of that love and support you have to give, it's matched only by the amount of scorn you are capable of showing if you feel disappointed, isn't it? If you don't see me living up to every detail of your fantasy from those moments in front of the television, under the blanket, in the darkness of the cinema. If that character you saw slinking across your screen, in that costume, in that role, is not the woman you see when you happen to stumble across her in the street in broad daylight or when you huddle together tightly at her stage door, jostling for a glimpse after a performance. God help her if she breaks that character you loved her for, if she pulls back the curtain or lets even the tiniest shard of clarity seep through when you meet her, when she politely requests some privacy at a lunch you've just interrupted. Watch the face. Watch the slow draining of the magic from those big, wide eyes you have. Watch that immense glow from the awe of having just seen the character of a painting step through the frame and into the gallery beside you, talk to you, touch you, watch that disappear as the realisation that their idol is just another woman in the world when we break that character. Feel that cascade through you as you learn that the painting was just a window into the other room after all. You hold all the love in your hands that we need, but that's what we hold in ours. And why if we are both seemingly forced to start off on a back foot together in this life, why is there so much scorn and ridicule when this disappointment happens? The nerve to still write and comment, complain and cancel each other so loudly and with so much passion and destruction. What is it that we owe each other? Or that you think we owe you? We are just vehicles for the characters of your dreams, we are not those women you see in your stories. We never were. It's just costumes and dialogue. Make up and lighting. Smoke and ice. The love you have is not for us, it's for the dream. It's like you're all running towards a cloud. You can see it in the distance and it's beautiful but when you're up there and you're face to face with it, it's all just air. None of it exists. But you still need us to fail to adore us. Why?' Veronica asked with a crack in her her voice. 'Why do you need that? Why do you need *me* to do that for you?' she shouted.

Just as she gestured towards herself with the hand holding the Oscar, letting it flop by her side mindlessly, suddenly the smooth gold statue slipped silently from her wet, trembling hand and fell to the floor with a heavy, metallic crash. The sound of it hitting the wood bounced about the empty stage and was followed instantly by the noise of it snapping into two with the pieces scattering clumsily about beneath her. Several loud gasps came from the darkness of the audience, along with the rustling of feet against carpet and clothing against the people as each of them, all at once, leant in to inspect it as best they could see from their seats.

Veronica was completely still. Her eyes were locked on the floor below her as she held her hands out with her palms open into the light. Short, panicked breaths that she took forced her body to twitch and twinkle with its sweat and sequins under the glare of the hot lamps, but still she didn't move.

When the noise of the tinny clash of the destroyed statue finally dissipated into the air around her and once the people were still in their seats again, she raised her head slowly to face them, swaying it from one end of the pit to the other, her eyes sprung wide open in utter devastation. She scanned around her, into the wings and out into the dark again, her mouth dropped and gaping, silently begging for help from anyone that may have been nearby to come and assist. But all the edges of the stage were empty and still.

Looking down again at the pieces below her, she eased onto her knees slowly and placed one hand on the gold body of the award that had rolled itself slowly to her toes and then one hand on the thick round base that had arrived slightly further to the right of her. She remained there crouching over herself in the spot light, holding the little segments like a child finding an upturned bird's nest from a tall tree, their gold coating glowing intensely under the hot white lights. And then finally she began to cry.

She pulled the pieces into her stomach, pressing them against her tightly as the tears in her eyes glistened in the light, falling from her face. The sobs sent her body into spasms each time she tried to breathe through them, her shoulders rising and shaking. She stuck a hand out to steady herself against the floor and appeared ready to try and brace herself to stand again, not realising however she had caught a section of her hair under her hand and so just as she rose herself up, the top stack of her wig began to slip. She twisted herself quickly about to stop it, placing an open palm over her head, but by the time she was fully upright, the wig had slid gently and silently from its position above her, falling slowly down her shoulder, dragging the bottom one with it also, both landing on the floor beside her in a dense, brown, wavy mass of nylon and netting.

Loud gasps from the audience poured in over her from the dark again, this time filled also with nervous moans of awkward pity. More and more little white laser lights from phones flickered on like a clumsy, mechanical constellation of stars with the rustling noises of people edging up and out of their seats growing louder. She gasped loudly, covering her mouth as best she could with the award still clenched tightly in her fist. Quickly she snapped herself down and snatched her hair pieces up again from their resting place at her feet, holding them tightly against her. But instead of trying to place it all back on her head, covering the exposed beige skull cap that was now beaming under the lights, all she seemed to be able to manage was to cradle it all together against her. Her sobs grew heavier, turning eventually into soft wails. 'Look what you've done now,' she said mostly mumbling through a shower of tears and a clogged throat looking down into her cradled arms. 'Look!'

She held up the golden figure in an outstretched arm and shoved it high into the beam of the spotlight. 'Look what you did to me now.' She pulled it back towards her chest and cried into the messy ball of wig hair as large ringlets of it flowed up over her arms and down her waist. As her cries grew louder, her body curled tighter in on itself and just as it seemed she would retreat almost entirely into a small crouching ball at the edge of the stage, she rose back up once more, pinned her shoulders back and extended her arm out to a sharp finger ending with the tipped blade of a nail directly into the silent crowd. 'I will not be your broken icon,' she screamed. 'You can't have me like this. I won't let you.'

She remained with her arm out for a moment, it shaking with a pain and rage that appeared to come from out in the dark and run through her hand and down her body. She pointed at nothing, at no one specifically, just a black mass of crawling shadows and tiny white lights. And still they were silent. The men out in there in the dark, saying nothing, just watching on as she melted gently down again towards the floor, folding her knees under herself and curving her body over, turning her cries into muffled sobs protected by her arms and hunched frame.

Slowly the bright lights of the stage dimmed, dousing her in a gentle darkness. For a brief moment she sat there sharing the shadows of the theatre together with the people watching on. But just as the silence that came with the dark began to slowly roll over them all, the ceiling above the seating sections simmered gently with a warm yellow glow, the strips of tiny runway lights that ran along the stairs towards the doors all shone brighter and the doors themselves were pulled in. Eventually the black mass that had sat so anonymously in the dark was suddenly alive and revealed. All their faces and clothes sitting under the rising sun of the theatre lights, exposed to each other.

But they didn't stand to shuffle themselves towards the exits, as the slow illuminating of their seats had suggested they do. They didn't gather their things or tousle with their coats and jackets and edge past each other awkwardly in the aisles. The moment the lights had finished their gentle dawning above them, the moment they were no longer the ones in the dark themselves, every person that had been sat there quietly, only watching, observing, rose to their feet and erupted into the loudest, most chaotic applause capable from a crowd that size. They whistled and stomped their feet and clapped, screamed and wailed all at once down towards Veronica as she lay curled up, still and alone on the darkened stage. It was the exact way that had harassed her from her room, the noise that had taunted her onto the stage in the first place, the deep, dull drumming of hundreds of feet against a floor and hands smacking one another, save for one difference. Peppered within their noise now was jubilant cheers and claps. Praise, not taunts. Applause not sneers. Several screams of an encore came through also. They stood there, all of them, not a single one still sitting or motioning to leave, rattling the structures of the theatre with their hysterical love for what they had just witnessed.

Eventually, Veronica peeked through the mass of synthetic hair her face had been pressed into and tried to focus at least one eye out before her at what was happening. Her face stung with the irritating mixture of her ruined make-up and salt from her eyes and her ears throbbed with the noise of her own distressed heart-beat. But still she watched, quietly captivated by the illuminated crowd as it jumped and danced about before her, whistling, film-ing, flashing from their phones, screaming her name, screaming to keep going and for more.

Confused and trembling slightly, she slowly rose to her feet, still clutching her wigs and pieces of the award tightly. As she did, the mania from the audience swelled, the pitch of the whistles climbed higher and their screams grew more frantic. She stood, glaring at the now glistening mass of bodies before her, sniffing and wiping the last of her rolling tears from her cheeks with the back of her hands, scanning them individually, locking her eyes into theirs as they smiled and waved up at her. They were men, as she had been told. Almost all men. Almost all older. Dressed in a certain way, combed and groomed in a certain way, standing and moving in a certain way. She surveyed them all as she could see them now from the circle down to the rows at her feet.

The spotlight appeared on her again, dousing her in its dusty cone and darkening her view of the crowd once more. It beamed down her entire body from the top of her still exposed head to the tail of her glistening gown flowing out behind her. She squinted directly into it, trying to shield her eyes with her arm, listening to the noises growing louder in the air around her. Some of the men she saw were now moving from their seats, edging their way across the rows and into the aisle, but not towards the doors or the exits. They moved towards her at the stage, walking quickly down the steep incline of the stairs and pouring into the space between her and the front row, clapping still and cheering as they did.

After scanning the scene before her once more, she finally allowed it to wash through her. She closed her eyes slowly, taking in each clap, each sound of her name, each noise of another person arriving from their seats to stand at her feet. As she did, she titled her face directly into the hot white light of the ceiling, pressed her eyes shut tighter and opened her mouth in a wide, ecstatic smile. She took a long, considered breath in through her nose and opened both her arms, one hand clutching both pieces of her broken Oscar, the other her mangled wigs, and just as she exhaled, she bowed elegantly towards the men out there in the dark, hanging there as their love and applause poured over her, louder than it had ever been before.

Printed in Great Britain
by Amazon